W9-BTK-241

"Suppose you and I were having an affair"

Patrick paused, holding her gaze. A million images flitted through her mind.

"It's hardly scandalous, is it?" he went on. "We're both of age and unattached. If there's a woman in my life, it doesn't raise eyebrows, and the same must apply to you. There must have been a man or two since you were widowed."

Darcie opened her mouth and shut it again.

His eyes narrowed. "No boyfriends at all?"

"No comment," she said frostily.

He gave a long drawn-out whistle. "You're a passionate woman. Three years is a long time to be on your own."

"Without a man, you mean," she said. "A typical male reaction. Why do men assume a widow is automatically pining for a man?"

"I'm not assuming," he said mildly. "*You* kissed *me*, remember?"

ANN CHARLTON, an Australian author, traces the beginning of her writing to a childhood period when, in trying to avoid nightmares, she began telling herself a story, continued each night. Her professional writing began with a short-story contest. Now she writes every weekday, interspersed with looking after her family. Tennis, sketching, reading, modern music and dancing are other interests. When both daughters have finished high school, Ann looks forward to travel and seeing new places.

Books by Ann Charlton

Don't miss any of our special offers. Write to us at the following address for information on our newest releases.

Harlequin Reader Service
901 Fuhrmann Blvd., P.O. Box 1397, Buffalo, NY 14240
Canadian address: P.O. Box 603,
Fort Erie, Ont. L2A 5X3

ANN CHARLTON

love spin

Harlequin Books

TORONTO • NEW YORK • LONDON
AMSTERDAM • PARIS • SYDNEY • HAMBURG
STOCKHOLM • ATHENS • TOKYO • MILAN

Harlequin Presents first edition December 1990
ISBN 0-373-11319-6

Original hardcover edition published in 1989
by Mills & Boon Limited

Copyright © 1989 by Ann Charlton. All rights reserved.
Except for use in any review, the reproduction or utilization
of this work in whole or in part in any form by any electronic,
mechanical or other means, now known or hereafter invented,
including xerography, photocopying and recording,
or in any information storage or retrieval system, is forbidden without
the permission of the publisher, Harlequin Enterprises Limited,
225 Duncan Mill Road, Don Mills, Ontario, Canada M3B 3K9.

All the characters in this book have no existence outside the
imagination of the author and have no relation whatsoever to
anyone bearing the same name or names. They are not even
distantly inspired by any individual known or unknown to the
author, and all incidents are pure invention.

® are Trademarks registered in the United States Patent and
Trademark Office and in other countries.

Printed in U.S.A.

CHAPTER ONE

DARCIE raced into the corner, holding off her brakes until the last possible moment to gain ground. Ahead of her, a Porsche clung to the track and ripped into the straight with a two-length lead she could not break. Sweat poured off her brow as she followed, trying to find the gap she needed in order to pass. But the Porsche driver was too good, too quick, and Darcie knew she might not make it. And she had to. Sweat rolled down her face and she thrust gloved fingers inside her visor to wipe away the moisture. She was seized by premonition. Something would happen if she didn't overtake the Porsche. If she could just get in front, then everything would be different.

She moved out in a right-hand feint behind the other car as they came to a corner. The Porsche driver swung out to cover the space, and moved quickly to cover the left as she attempted a double-feint to get past. She came close behind, almost in his slipstream, and the premonition closed in on her split seconds before it all went wrong. The driver in front lost it and his car slewed, then ran off the track kicking up dust and smoke from the tyre. The Porsche rolled and rolled again. Darcie saw the spurt of flame and suddenly, shockingly, she knew why she had been trying to overtake and change the sequence, knew who was in the car.

'Gavin!' she screamed as the Porsche went up in flames and smoke. 'Get out. Get out!' she screeched, tears rolling down inside her helmet. Then, as she looked back over her shoulder, she lost control of her own car, went into a spin, and ploughed through a crowd barrier, scattering white-faced people. A child screamed and went on screaming . . .

By the time Darcie turned the Toyota into Ensigns' underground car park she was tense and already tired. Partly because of Sydney's peak morning traffic, but mostly because of the dream.

Tucking her chauffeur's cap under her arm, she made her way to the fleet office. Bill Trimble was the only driver there, and he regarded her with scarcely veiled antagonism. There were three reasons for this: one, she was the first woman driver to penetrate this male bastion, two, she was a close friend of Ensigns' managing director, and three—and worst of all—she had failed to respond to Bill's flashy good looks and sex appeal, which he rated very highly. It might, she thought, have soothed Bill's ego to know that she hadn't responded to any man for the past three years, and wasn't likely to.

'You're to pick up Stafford in ten minutes,' Bill told her. 'Side entrance.'

'Patrick Stafford? Mark's—I mean, Mr Rawlinson's nephew? I thought *you* were to be his regular driver.'

'So did I. But your very good friend *Mark*——' he emphasised the first name with a sneer'—rang through himself and gave orders that *you* were to have that plum job in future. Nice to be bosom buddies with the MD. You'll have to take the Rolls,' he finished, with the sulky look of a child separated from a prized toy.

'Sorry. I know how that hurts,' she said lightly, ignoring the innuendo. 'I'll nurse her along and bring her back without a scratch.'

Darcie went to the mirror and straightened her cap while Bill lounged against the table, giving her some patronising advice on how to handle the Rolls. She listened with her usual air of polite attention, amused that the male drivers thought it necessary to instruct her. If only they knew, she thought. Wryly she regarded her reflection. Gold-brown hair neatened into a roll to suit the cap, the minimum of make-up, cheekbones a mite too defined, skin too pale, perhaps, eyes too blue against the pallor. An average, nice-looking sort of woman, she observed. All the rest was ancient history. What was there to know?

There were two men talking at the side entrance of Ensigns, and Darcie wondered if one of them was her passenger. When one of them glanced at his watch and looked around she nodded to him, got out, and stood by the back passenger door. He looked much as she had expected Mark's nephew to look. Mark and his sister were fraternal twins—alike, but no more so than any brother and sister. This young man was tall and slim like his uncle and mother and, also like them, impeccably dressed. Dark, three-piece suit, hair fashionably cut and well groomed. Quite good-looking. She watched him make a point emphatically to the other, scruffy-looking man.

Patrick did not see eye to eye with his family, she gathered, but Mark had always spoken of him with avuncular tolerance. That tolerance had swiftly dissipated when Patrick made it clear that, after ten years of seeking his own fortune here and abroad, he wanted an active part in the running of Ensigns before, as he was quoted as saying, 'the company expired'. Mark and his sister, the major shareholders, closed ranks against this implied criticism of them both, and did their best to keep Patrick out. But he, too, was a major shareholder since he'd bought out a third cousin and a disinterested great-aunt, and Patrick was therefore *in*. A very peculiar way for a man to treat his own mother and uncle, Darcie thought, business or no business.

She opened the door smartly as the good-looking newcomer came forward. But though he paused, glanced her way and smiled, he skirted around the Rolls and stepped out on to the road to hail a taxi. Darcie, staring after him, swung the door closed and hit something. There was a muffled grunt of pain. She snatched the door open again—not *something*, but *someone*.

'Good lord, man, what's the matter with you?' a testy voice said close by, and she looked down to see the other man bend to rub his shin and pick up a dropped file. The *other* man? The burly one with the untidy hair and no looks to speak of, and the sports jacket that looked as if it had spent all night on a park bench? This couldn't be Mark's nephew, elegant Barbara Stafford's son. She crouched down to help gather up the sheets of paper that had fluttered from the file. The man's gaze homed in on her legs, then raised abruptly to her face.

'You're a woman!'

The man was brilliant, she thought. 'Yes, sir.' She shuffled several pages together and handed them to him.

'I didn't know we had any women drivers.'

'Just one, sir,' she said. Even the voice was wrong. Rough-textured, abrupt. Mark Rawlinson had grace and finesse. She had assumed that, whatever else he might lack, his expensively educated nephew would have some too. He stood up and so did she.

'I don't like women drivers,' he informed her.

She met his eyes steadily. 'I see, Mr Stafford.'

'Too emotional. They talk too much.'

He got into the car and she closed the door. Another chauvinist. Well, who cared? 'Where to, Mr Stafford?' she asked from the driver's seat.

He wanted to go to the factory. 'You do know where the factory is, I hope?' he said drily as she started the Rolls. 'Or do you only take the fashionable route between here and the best restaurants and hotels?'

It was a shrewd guess and an indictment of certain well-fed Ensigns executives, but it implied criticism of the drivers and Darcie felt that was below the belt. Drivers only went where they were told. In the rear-view mirror she could see him, intent on some paperwork which was spread out over the attaché case across his knees. He periodically punched the buttons on a defenceless calculator. So women drivers talked too much, did they? she thought, both annoyed and amused. He would find there were exceptions. She had strict rules of non-involvement with her passengers. She liked the anonymity of the uniform and the impersonal 'sir' which seemed to appeal to middle-management egos.

He reached over and opened the sliding glass divider behind her head. 'What's the petrol consumption on this showpiece?'

Darcie blinked. 'Sorry—what do you——?'

'The Rolls,' he explained, as if she were slow-witted. 'How much petrol does it use per week?'

She recovered, and gave him an estimate at which he whistled.

'Madness!' he muttered. 'Can't see how we can justify that. What's a Rolls got that we couldn't get from an L.T.D? Tell me that—what's your name?'

'Darcie, sir.'

'Ms Darcy . . . well?'

'I'm sorry, sir. I thought the question was rhetorical,' she said evenly. 'A Rolls has the best motor in the world, possibly the quietest. Comfort. Nil devaluation, prestige——'

'Ah, yes, prestige!' he snorted. 'We're very big on prestige in Ensigns. Imported cars, underworked chauffeurs playing poker to pass the time. All prestige and no bread and butter.' He looked up suddenly, and met her startled eyes in the rear-view mirror. 'But don't start any panics among the drivers, will you? Your jobs aren't in jeopardy. Only the Rolls, OK?' He went back to punishing the calculator. 'I have a report to write. Keep her nice and steady, Ms Darcy. Can you manage that?'

'I'll try, sir,' she said, piqued by the undisguised doubt in his voice.

She reached around to close the partition, wondering whether to tell him he was using her first name and not her last, when he muttered without looking up, 'If you're going to shut that thing, for Pete's sake, do it! No one in this company seems able to make a decision from the chauffeur upwards.'

Darcie shut the screen with a decisive little snap. At the Silverwater factory, Patrick Stafford took his attaché case and clipboard and strode off with a backflung, 'I'll be half an hour.'

She watched him go. He was a bit under six feet, she assessed, and built like a tank. She revised her opinion of his clothes. They didn't look as if he'd slept in them, they looked as if he'd been to *war* in them. His predicted half-hour at the factory turned out to be closer to an hour, and improved his mood no end. He was whistling as he came out. Darcie had the Rolls door open for him, wide open. She wasn't taking any chances of a repeat accident. He stopped to consider her stiff, Grenadier guard-like stance by the open door.

'A woman who profits by her mistakes. I like that.' He grinned and she almost jumped at the change. His big, rugged teeth were white and strong. All the better to eat you up with, my dear. Nevertheless, they enhanced his smile, which was unexpectedly attractive, softening the hard-edged lines in his cheeks. The sudden transformation made her aware of other things about him. His grey eyes were thickly lashed and one opened rather wider than the other, his nose looked as if it had met with some opposition once or twice, and his mouth, altogether too thin for its width, looked a whole lot better in humour. She couldn't think when she'd seen such an asymmetrical face. Nothing matched anything else. Especially the eyes. His eyes made her inexplicably uneasy.

'Maybe I won't have to wear shin-guards after all,' he mocked.

'No, sir,' she said, and concentrated on getting him and the Rolls back to Ensigns without a scratch.

She ended the day as she'd begun it, tense and tired. Sleep was slow to come, and in the early hours of the morning she dreamed again. It happened that way. For months she could be free of it, then it would plague her for two, three, four nights in a row, taking her relentlessly around the nightmare racetrack, where she was unable to change the sequence of events.

On mornings after the dream she felt almost sick at the thought of driving a car—even one so ordinary as her fourteen-year-old Toyota. Darcie fought the fear with a fierce concentration on minor tasks—anything to postpone driving till the last possible moment. She wiped the kitchen counters over for a second time. She cut some roses from the garden, arranged them, and moved the vase from here to there until she ·was satisfied. She pinned up the latest postcard from her parents on the kitchen notice-board. The view of Alice Springs joined a letter from her younger brother, and a photo of him and his young, very pregnant wife, standing in the garden of their newly acquired house in Mackay. Her older brother had embraced yuppiedom in Canberra. The photograph of him included his girlfriend and his Alfa Romeo, both new. Darcie spent some time at the notice-board, wishing her family was not so scattered, then she made tea and toast for Matt and took it in to him.

'Matt,' she called softly, putting down the tray in his room. There was no movement from the anonymous jumble of bedclothes and T-shirts and jeans and odd socks. Matt's socks always entered the house in pairs, and were never seen together again. Darcie picked up a thin blue and a thick white sock and looked around for any mates. None. From the floor she collected two record covers, a text-book on accountancy and his leather bike-jacket, from the pockets of which showered combs, coins, his college ID card and his best friend's driving licence. Piling these on a chair, she dropped the socks back on to the unmoving, sheet-shrouded body, giving a little shake where she supposed a shoulder to be. 'Matt.' He didn't move. Darcie looked at her watch, grimacing. She couldn't postpone it any longer. It was time to go and face the Toyota. She tried to walk out without looking at the picture on the wall, but at the last moment her eyes lifted to the life-sized poster. The man in it laughed at her. He wore a red driving-suit and had laurel leaves around his neck. He leaned on a Formula One Porsche and, behind him, champagne spouted from a shaken bottle. Victory at Monza. The man was striking: coal-black, curly hair, vital tanned skin, and brown eyes ablaze with triumph. It was a magnificent picture of a man in his prime, caught in a moment of elation when the world was his and only his. Gavin. Husband, lover, friend. Just one more race, he'd said, then he would retire on his thirty eighth birthday. There was a small stone cross beside the track at Hockenheim to mark the finish of Gavin's last race. She hated the poster.

'Get up, Matt. You'll be late for school.'

The bedclothes heaved. Matt sat up in bed and yawned. He had coal-black hair and brows and tanned skin. Gavin's son was a poignant younger copy.

'I brought you some tea and toast,' said Darcie.

'I wish you wouldn't cut the toast into four bits,' he grumbled, taking one of the dainty triangular segments.

'I've been cutting your toast like that since you were eleven.'

'My mouth's bigger now.' He disposed of the triangle

in one mouthful to prove his point. 'And I don't go to school any more. College, that's where I go. You know, that school for *big* boys and girls?' He thrust another piece of toast into his mouth.

'Don't talk with your mouth full. Did I say "school"?' she said lightly. 'Force of habit.' She said 'school' to tease him, but sometimes she guiltily wondered if it was another of her delaying tactics. Just as she sometimes tried to postpone going out to the car, she might be trying to postpone, or at least slow down, Matt's approach to adulthood. A schoolboy stepson had been so much more comfortable to deal with, for all the wild arguments over liberty and pocket-money. She studied him while he gulped some tea. Matt had a spattering of acne along his chin and jaw, which stubbornly refused to respond to treatment. Was that a bruise on his neck? Or could it be a love-bite?

'Can I borrow the car tonight, Darcie?' he asked as she found two more socks and examined them for signs of brotherhood.

'You're taking Roberta out again?'

He gave a sort of a grunt, which she took for assent. 'That mark on your neck, Matt . . .'

His hand flew to cover it. Jerkily, he pulled up the sheet to shroud his bare shoulder. 'What about it?'

'Is it a love-bite?' she asked, wondering just how far this friendship with Roberta had gone. The girl was only just seventeen, after all.

Matt burst out laughing. 'Come on, Darcie—it would be some kind of a record, a love-bite that size!'

'It's a bruise, then. How did you hurt yourself like that?'

His laughter went, leaving him secretive and

brooding. He shrugged, avoiding her eyes.

'You must have done something.' She flicked the sheet aside and saw that his back, too, was bruised. 'Matt, you're *covered* in bruises——' Her heartbeat quickened. How many times had she seen Gavin bruised and bandaged? Or herself, for that matter? She rejected the images.

'So what?' He snatched the sheet back and hunched his shoulder into it. 'I'm not a little kid any more, Darcie. I don't come running to you for a plaster every time I bruise myself in a shunt.'

A *shunt*. Darcie gave a start at the racing jargon. Matt held up a hasty hand at the look of horror on her face.

'Look, I—skidded, fell off my bike, OK? It happens.'

Darcie took a deep breath, but he anticipated her.

'Yeah, yeah, I *was* wearing my helmet, no, I *hadn't* partaken of any alcoholic beverage, yeah, I *will* be more careful in future.'

She smiled. 'Am I such a nag?'

'It's a foul job, but someone's got to do it.' Matt grinned. 'So, can I have the car tonight?'

'Yes, all right. Make sure you take Roberta home on time tonight, won't you? And . . .' She hesitated, and Matt looked up wickedly beneath his black brows.

'And don't do anything *you* wouldn't do?' he mocked. 'Give me a break, Darcie, I have to live a *little*.'

She blinked. 'And I don't?'

'You might call it living, listening to brass bands with Mr Personality, but I don't.'

'I happen to quite like brass bands, and Gary is a very nice man,' she defended half-heartedly.

'Nice and boring. He's looking for a nursemaid for his kids. Why don't you tell him to get lost?'

'Because I'm not seventeen and arrogant and rude, that's why.'

'Neither am I. I'm *eighteen* and arrogant and rude.'

'Seventeen-and-a-half and arrogant and rude.' She tossed the licence-folder to him. 'This fell out of your jacket pocket. Chris is probably wondering where it got to. How on earth do you happen to have his driver's licence, anyway?'

Matt looked startled, then angry. He flushed a deep red.

'Hell, Darcie, are you going through my pockets now?'

'You know that's not my style. It fell out when I picked your jacket up off the floor,' she said, stung by the accusation. She never spied on him, checked his pockets or read his mail. *Never.* 'If you're so sensitive about your clothes, maybe you should try hanging them up occasionally. And I wish you wouldn't swear!' She tossed the pair of odd socks on to his bed and walked out.

A little later he emerged, dressed in regulation student gear of jeans, T-shirt and jacket, his satchel slung over one arm. 'Sorry, Darcie,' he said, looking conscience-stricken. 'I know you don't pry. Just the opposite, really, otherwise you would have . . . Well, sorry.'

He watched her push the vase of roses to the left of the gleaming sideboard, then to the right. 'You cried out in your sleep again last night,' he said.

'Oh, I dreamed something stupid—about lizards. You know how I feel about lizards,' she said with a shudder, aware that she wasn't fooling Matt. She gathered up her cap and keys. 'Well, another day. I wonder if I'll have to drive the charming Patrick again today.'

'You've met him, then?'

'I've been assigned as his regular driver—something I intend to change as soon as I can beard Mark in his office.'

'He's that bad?'

'Rude, abrupt, chauvinistic, and no respect for tradition. The Rolls is on his hit-list, and there's a rumour that he's going to commit the company to a new public image—sponsor a football team or something, to promote some new line of sports goods. Can you imagine it? Ensigns Prestige Leathergoods getting involved with sweaty team sports? Mark will fight tooth and nail against it. Trouble is,' she said thoughtfully, 'I can't see anyone stopping Stafford if he decides on a course of action.'

'Aggressive, is he?' Matt asked, equally thoughtfully.

'Think of any army tank with guns blazing.'

The description was sound, she thought, as she opened the door later for Stafford. He bore down on her and barked out his destination.

'Good morning, sir,' she said, dubiously casting an eye over his beige trousers, tweedy sports jacket, and khaki wool tie which was slightly off-centre. A man in a hurry, she thought. And that was being charitable.

In the rear-view mirror all she could see was the top of his head as he played back a message on a tiny tape recorder. He had thick, rather coarse brown hair which looked as if he'd been in a battle, or as if a very energetic, passionate woman had run her hands through it for a couple of hours. Darcie suppressed a laugh. More likely a battle. He didn't look the type to inspire passion in women. They might feel impelled to press his trousers or straighten that awful tie, but make love to him? The traffic lights were red, and, rather startled by the trend of her thoughts, she studied him overtly. When he looked up suddenly, their eyes met in the mirror. He reached over and opened the partition.

'I believe green means "go",' he said.

'Sir?'

'The lights, Ms Darcy. The lights.'

Chagrined, and just a bit flustered, she stepped on the accelerator and the Rolls surged forward like a liner on the crest of a tidal wave. Patrick Stafford's tape recorder bounced from his knee.

'Sorry, sir.'

'Hell, I hate women drivers!'

The man brought out the worst in her, Darcie admitted after another week. Her driving seemed to go to pieces when Stafford sat in the back, totting up figures and scribbling reports. The man would never believe her if she told him who she was, she thought, baffled and aggravated by her poor performance.

'Good lord!' he exclaimed one day as she jerked around a corner and his paperwork slid across the seat. 'I'm beginning to wonder if the rumours about you are true.'

'Sorry, sir?' she said. 'Rumours, sir?'

'I wish you wouldn't parrot my key words. You sound like the butler out of an old English movie. And don't say "butler, sir?" for heaven's sake!' There was an irate rustle as he picked up his papers. 'You must know the rumours I mean.' He emerged from the floor area and looked directly at her eyes in the rear-view mirror. That lopsided stare of his could be very disturbing. One eye was wide open and coldly assessing, the other was almost languid, amused, suggestive beneath its slightly drooping lid. No wonder the upper echelon were in confusion. When they sat on his right, they knew he was a hard man, but when they sat on his left they could be fatally fooled.

'The grapevine has it that my uncle only hired you because you're his girlfriend,' he said bluntly. 'I didn't think you looked the type, but your lousy driving forces me to consider the possibility.'

Her face flamed. Any reply she might have made was forestalled as he slammed the divider shut with a careless sweep of one big hand, and applied himself to a phone call.

Darcie was furious. She wasn't sure why she should be so incensed this time, for the rumours, after all, had drifted around since Mark had hired her. But the way Patrick Stafford had brought the matter up raked across her pride and rankled for hours afterwards. He had no sensitivity. No class. No taste. But she held her tongue and kept her feelings more or less under control—all but her frustration at his appearance. He was a successful man—he'd startled his own computer software business and sold it at a handy profit, according to Mark, and had been a troubleshooter for two large American companies. Successful and well paid. So how come he didn't look it?

When she delivered him to the Sebel Townhouse one day, where he was to meet his counterpart from a client company, her rule of non-involvement failed her. The client, Darcie knew, was a meticulous man. Heaven knew what Mr Moxham would think of Patrick Stafford's careless appearance! At the hotel she opened the Rolls door and, as he emerged, she held out a comb.

'Mr Stafford?'

'What's this?'

'A comb, sir.'

'So I see.' He made no move to take it.

'It's clean,' she assured him. 'Brand new, in fact.'

'Fascinating,' he said, 'but why are you giving it to me?'

Her eyes lifted speakingly to his hair. She knew now why it so frequently looked mussed. He had a habit of dragging a hand through it while he concentrated on his paperwork. 'Maybe if you used the mirror . . .' she suggested, and walked along to the wing mirror, tilting it for him. He came and peered into it. With a grudging sort of grunt, and a piercing look at her, he took the comb and used it.

'There,' he said mockingly. 'Do I pass?'

But Darcie's attention had already turned to his suit. From the car she produced her own clothes-brush. 'If you'll allow me, sir,' she said, and set to energetically to remove the tiny bits of lint that clung to his jacket.

Darcie felt him watching her, but kept her eyes on what she was doing, walking around him to do his back. It made quite an area to cover, she found. The man really *was* built like a tank under that jacket. Maybe that was why it sat so badly on him; slim, lean men could look elegant in their clothes, but elegance would always escape Patrick Stafford.

'Over and above the duties of a driver, isn't it, Ms Darcy?' he said over his shoulder.

'I'm just an underworked chauffeur, sir, trying to fill in time. I don't like poker.'

He laughed and his jacket strained across his shoulders. He was considerably taller than she'd first thought. Because he was built on such broad lines, it tended to disguise his height. This was about the closest she'd been to him without a car door between them, and Darcie had to look up. He was over six feet in height, she reassessed. His grey eyes were alert as they flicked over her.

'Finished?'

Her eyes fell to his tie. Darcie told herself that she'd gone too far already, but tidying him up was proving addictive. She couldn't stop herself. Clamping the clothes-brush under her arm, she centred his tie and adjusted the knot. He was pleasantly warm through the shirt, the upper reaches of his chest as hard as a rock beneath the heels of her hands. An illusion, very likely. Big men in desk-jobs ran to flab very fast. She stepped back when she'd finished.

'You wouldn't like to polish my boots too, would you?' he asked, amused.

'Lick them, you mean?' she retorted before she could stop herself. She compressed her lips. 'Sorry.'

Eyes narrowed, he slotted the comb half into the breast-pocket of her uniform shirt. 'You're not quite the docile yes-man I thought.' His eyes lingered on the curve of her breast beneath the pocket. 'Yes-*woman*,' he corrected softly, and let the comb drop. His rough voice had a husky quality when pitched so low. Suede over shell-grit, she thought, surprised to find that she liked it. She removed the comb and held it out to him. 'Keep it,' she said sincerely. 'Please.'

His eyes narrowed, and a cool breeze blew in from somewhere.

'Has my dapper uncle given you the job of bringing me up to scratch? Is that what's brought on this sudden solicitude?'

'No, he has not,' Darcie said, stiffening at his sarcastic reference to Mark. 'I'm acting entirely on my own initiative.'

'Ah.' The cool breeze departed. He fingered the knot of his tie and smiled slightly as he studied her. 'I'm not normally so disorganised. My housekeeper tossed it in after a couple of days. I'm looking for a new one.'

It explained why he looked faintly dishevelled, she supposed. What surprised her was that he bothered to give an explanation. 'I hope you find one soon, sir,' she said earnestly.

'Cut the "sir" stuff,' he said. 'It might go down well with the old guard here, but as far as I'm concerned the inimitable Jeeves went out with gaiters.'

'Whatever you say, Mr Stafford. Mr Moxham is expecting you in five minutes. Was there anything else?'

'You could have dinner with me tonight.'

Darcie gaped. 'Dinner?' She felt a tremendous force build up behind her refusal, too much for her own peace of mind. It was only a dinner invitation, and a 'no-frills' one at that. None the less, her pulse-rate quickened. 'Thanks, but no thanks.'

He reached for her left hand, checking out her ringless fingers. 'Not married, not engaged. So why not?'

Sheer arrogance. As if the only possible reason for refusing him would be that she was already taken.

'I don't believe in mixing business with pleasure,' she said. He raised a brow, as if he thought this was less than an excuse, and she was impelled to add, 'I don't think staff should fraternise with management.' His other brow went up. 'And—um—I have to . . .'

'Wash your hair?' he drawled. 'If you've run out of

clichés, tell me the real reason.'

What an aggravating man! Darcie began to think he would stand here all day unless she offered him a reason he could believe. 'All right,' she snapped, 'I don't like you.' Darcie's eyes flew wide open. She was hardly able to believe she'd said that. Stafford's own gritty directness must be catching. 'What I mean is—um . . .'

'Don't embroider. I asked, and you gave me your answer. I like that. Your honesty, that is, not the actual answer,' he said drily. 'Perhaps you'll change your mind.'

'I don't think so. I rarely accept dinner invitations, Mr Stafford.'

'Perhaps you'll change your mind about that, too.'

Too? Darcie worked it out. Was he saying that she might get to like him? What was there to like? The male ego was truly boundless. Darcie lifted her eyes to his again. There were a host of signals to be read there. On the left, amusement, warmth, interest, a certain earthiness. On the right, cool assessment, calculation, determination. Take your pick. Darcie didn't care for either side. And she cared even less for the combination.

CHAPTER TWO

THERE was a pervading, pleasant smell of new leather in Mark's outer office, where some of Ensigns' most beautiful leathergoods were showcased. His inner office was elegant, furnished with antiques, a Persian rug and restored Edwardian lamps. Widowed ten years before, Mark had never found anyone who could replace his wife. He had taken her hobby as his own and expanded her cherished antique collection ever since. Darcie often thought that a little bit of Marie Rawlinson lived in every piece he bought. Mark's office was a study in timelessness and tranquillity at any time. Seen like this, at six in the evening, with the building quiet, the main lighting off and only the glow of the lamps, it radiated serenity.

Mark did not, however. He looked drawn and harried, and Darcie felt a surge of resentment against his nephew, the cause of it. Mark wasn't surprised when she asked to be taken off the regular run as Stafford's driver.

'Wine, my dear?' He poured some wine into fine, crystal goblets. 'Has he upset you, too?'

'I wish you hadn't elevated me to the job. The other drivers don't like me being singled out. It has revived all those stupid rumours about me being your kept woman and getting all the plum jobs as a result.'

Mark made sympathetic noises and asked her casually where she had driven Patrick lately, and if she'd heard him talking to anyone in particular on the carphone. Darcie offered one or two observations and, embarrassed, came to a halt.

'Mark, did you assign me as his driver to spy on him?'

'He could prove a most disruptive force,' Mark said with the faint, aggrieved tone of one trying to justify himself. 'He's impatient and thinks he knows everything, the young pipsqueak! He wants us to switch to cheap gym-bags and chain-store stuff to the detriment of our prestige lines, and those lines are what made this company. It would help me to know what he's up to.'

'But to *spy* on him?'

He had a stubborn look about him that amazed Darcie. She couldn't remember Mark behaving like this. For the first time it occurred to her that all the fault might not lie with Stafford.

'As a favour to me, Darcie,' Mark said.

There was no denying she owed Mark a favour. She had known him since she was fourteen, when he and Marie built a weekend cabin alongside her parents' farm. Mark and Marie, whose tastes had run to art and opera and other gentle pursuits, had nevertheless come to watch her churn up mud in her first race, a hill sprint. She had cried at Marie's funeral; Mark had smiled at Darcie's wedding, comforted her in her grief. What had started as a pleasant, neighbourly association had been cemented into friendship by shared celebration and pain. Mark's sympathy and understanding had helped her get through the past few years. He had offered her this job, and she was grateful.

'Your nephew's thinking of getting rid of the Rolls,'

she told Mark lightly. 'That's about the most anarchistic piece of news I can pass on at present.'

Mark didn't laugh. He appeared to have lost all sense of humour as far as Patrick was concerned. Eventually, though, after another glass of wine, he relaxed and asked about Matt's studies.

'And does he ever talk about racing these days?'

Darcie's laugh was pitched a fraction too high. 'No, that phase is over, thank heavens! I suppose all boys fancy themselves as a racing driver at some time or other. Or a pop star, or an astronaut.'

Mark looked at her thoughtfully over his wine glass. 'And yet Matt is not quite like *all* boys who fantasise, is he? I mean, not many boys have a Grand Prix champion for a father and Darcie Miller for a stepmama.'

'Darcie Brooke,' she said rather stiltedly. 'I may not wear my wedding ring any more, but I'm still Darcie Brooke.'

'Did you know that Matt asked me once if Ensigns would sponsor him?'

Darcie's fingers tightened convulsively around the glass.

'No. When?'

'Over a year ago. I didn't tell you because I knew you'd be upset. Naturally I told him no—that Ensigns didn't feel sport sponsorship suited its image. Something else Patrick wants to change.' His mouth tightened at the thought. 'And I gave Matt a lecture on the ephemeral nature of racing as against, say, engineering or medicine or accountancy. Of course, he was only sixteen at the time, and seemed rather vague about what kind of vehicles he would race if he had the chance, so I suppose it was merely a whim, as you say.'

'Thank heavens he went to you!' Darcie said shakily. 'Someone else might have encouraged him just because he's Gavin Brooke's son.' She laid a hand on his arm, and removed it in a hurry when Mark drew in a rather sharp breath. He rubbed at his midriff and grimaced.

'Lobster for lunch,' he said dolefully. 'It never agrees with me.'

'Why order it, then?'

'Sheer greed.'

Laughing, she took his arm again. 'Thank you, Mark.'

'For what, my dear?'

'For talking sense to Matt. You're a real friend.' She leaned close and kissed his cheek, and as she did so someone walked into the office. Darcie straightened up quickly.

With his sleeves rolled up, an open file in his hands, Patrick halted just inside the door. He looked at his uncle, then hard at Darcie. He checked out their cosy pairing on the settee, the two wine glasses, the low lights.

'Mixing business with pleasure after all, Ms Darcy?' he said sardonically. 'I can see you're busy, Mark. You should close the door when you're—er—*interviewing* the chauffeur.'

The door closed behind him with a contemptuous little snick. Darcie bit her lip, mortified, then angry. No doubt he construed her surprise as guilt. 'I'm sick to death of people misreading things. You will tell him he's wrong, won't you, Mark?'

And Mark said of course he would tell him. Couldn't have the boy jumping to conclusions and making a fool of himself, which was so patently what Mark *would* like that she left, out of all patience with him *and* his nephew.

Stafford hardly looked at her in the morning when she picked him up. But at his destination he expected to be brushed down. It was, apparently, to be part of the job from now on. Darcie wished she'd never given in to the urge to tidy him up.

'What do you do in your spare time?' he asked, watching her briskly buff at his left sleeve. 'Apart from keeping my uncle young and helping him spend the dwindling company profits?'

'I grow roses,' she said shortly.

'That's it?' he mocked. 'Roses? No night-life? I mean, you can't spend *every* evening with Uncle, unless of course you're totally absorbed with antiques, too.' He gave her a moment to appreciate the *double entendre*. She concentrated on his lapels. 'No parties, Ms Darcy? No dancing till dawn? No nude sunbathing?' Doggedly she ignored him, and he gave a dry laugh. 'No, I guess not. You realise that, as an old man's darling, you really don't fit the mould. Not obvious enough. So—apart from my uncle and growing roses, how do you spend your time?'

'I'm a part-time mud-wrestler!' she snapped.

He gave a snort of laughter. 'What's your first name?'

'Jezebel.'

Another bark of laughter was followed by one of those double-barrelled, ambiguous looks that could have meant anything at all. Darcie adjusted his tie. It was even lousier than usual. Cerise and blue Paisley.

'Finished, sir.' She stepped back, the perfect valet. 'And may I say how *very* well your tie suits you, sir.'

She had the satisfaction of seeing him uncertain. He glanced down at the tie, frowned at her, and told her to come back for him in a hour. As he walked away Darcie saw him take the end of the tie in one hand and give it some close scrutiny.

Gary Norris knocked at her door only minutes after she arrived home on Wednesday night. Matt was right about Gary. Their neighbour was nice, but boring. He was divorced with two children in his custody, and saw himself and Darcie as kindred spirits. He dropped in often with home-grown produce and invitations to listen to his collection of brass-band recordings. She'd gone once, hounded into it by choruses of 'Please come to our house, *please!*' from his irresistible children, and she'd been manufacturing excuses not to repeat the experience ever since. However, considering the bounty he had brought her on this occasion, she felt it would be downright unneighbourly not to ask him in.

'Saw Matt's double in the paper last Monday,' Gary told her while she poured some fruit juice for his children 'Looked just like him.'

Darcie smiled. 'If it was his double, I suppose it would.'

'Amazingly like him, in fact,' Gary plodded on.

He had no sense of humour, Darcie despaired, but a tremendous sense of purpose. Gary never left a subject until he had worried it to death.

'Wasn't him, of course. A trick of the light. The fellow's face was in shadow because he was wearing a . . .'

Some spilled orange juice claimed Darcie's attention as Gary droned on. '. . . the fellow's name was Christopher something-or-other—I'll think of it in a minute . . .'

But he didn't think of it, and, after some desultory discussion about his runner beans and her roses, he rounded up his children and went home.

On Thursday night Matt came home, his mood swinging wildly between elation and brooding.

'You must be in love,' she joked. Several times he appeared on the verge of some confidence, but changed his mind. Darcie crossed her fingers. Just don't let him be enamoured of a punk-rocker, she thought, but someone nice like Roberta.

In the morning Matt was up early, even before Darcie. He woke her with tea and toast. 'Time I repaid the favour,' he said when she sat up in amazement. 'I've cut the toast into poncy little bits the way you like.' He grinned at her glance of reproval. 'Um—I have to go, Darcie. I'll probably stay over at Chris's place for the weekend, OK?' He dropped a kiss on her forehead, then bounded to the door while Darcie was still stuttering on a batch of 'buts'.

'Chris's place? But you're always over there. You should invite Chris here more often. It isn't fair on Mrs Reynolds, having you there eating her out of house and home——'

'Yeah, yeah—I'll take her some chocolates, right?'

'But——'

But Matt was gone. His bike roared jubilantly down the drive as she opened the front door. 'Bye, Matt,' she said wryly to herself. Then she picked up the rolled newspaper from the front lawn, pulled a few dead heads from a Roundelay rose-bush, and went in.

It was an ordinary Friday morning. The Sorensons' dog barked and the canary next door whistled and the

Lewis children two doors down called goodbye to their father in high piccolo voices, 'Bye, Daddy, bye-bye . . .'

Darcy spread some marmalade on the toast Matt had made for her and unrolled the newspaper, pausing when a name on the sports page caught her eye. It was 'Stafford'—a common enough name. She scowled that it should light up like a neon sign for her in the sea of words and names. Dismissively she passed it over, but her eye was drawn back by another familiar name. 'Ensigns'. Both appeared in a short paragraph headed 'Have Goods Will Travel'.

> With significant sponsorship for motor racing thin on the ground these days, young touring-class amateur, Chris Reynolds, might pull off a deal with Ensigns, manufacturers and importers of travel goods. Promising youngster Reynolds, eighteen, has had drives in only eight WSTCC races, and been placed in five. Neither he nor Mr P.A. Stafford of Ensigns was available for comment.

Darcie read and re-read the piece, growing more unsettled each time. Ensigns becoming involved in racing was too close for comfort. Why couldn't Stafford have pinned his promotions on a football team as everyone expected? Chris Reynolds. Same name as Matt's friend. Funny that they'd just been talking about Chris . . . Darcie sat there, her teacup raised while the ordinary Friday-morning sounds filtered through the windows. The canary next door trilled and a garage door crashed shut and Mrs Lewis called her children in from the gate. A number of facts slid into place in her mind.

Matt's best friend was called Chris Reynolds.

Chris's driving licence had fallen out of Matt's pocket. *A driving licence.*

The tea tilted in her cup. World champion Jackie Stewart had raced as an amateur and kept it a secret from his parents. And his son Paul had used a friend's licence to go to driving school at Brand's Hatch . . . there were countless stories like that in racing. A friend's licence for an under-age driver, or for one who wanted to keep his real name quiet. Darcie tried to back off from it. It was an ordinary name, after all. There must be dozens of people around called Chris Reynolds. A pulse made itself felt on her temple. More facts fell into line.

Matt and his evasions. Matt and his secrecy, his annoyance whenever she questioned him, which she'd put down to irritable adolescence. Matt asking Mark if Ensigns would sponsor him one day. Matt studying weekend after weekend at Chris's place, or in the library, and only just scraping passes in his exams. Matt bruised from a 'shunt'. Fell off the bike, he'd said. But what if . . .? No. Darcie sat frozen, her teacup raised and motionless. A shunt. Gavin's last shunt had killed him. 'Oh, no.' She shook her head. Matt was going to be an accountant. He wasn't going to get involved in the crazy, cruel game of racing. He'd gone through a silly stage, but he'd lost interest in it, as she knew he would if he was just left alone. But she remembered now how thoughtful he'd been when she had spoken about Stafford and his plan for a new Ensigns image, and all her rationalisation couldn't stem the fear. There was something else. Something else. A name the same as Matt's best friend and—what? Darcie remembered. She downed her cup, slopping tea on the table, and ran to the bedroom. She threw on her uniform skirt and blouse, and went across the road to Gary's house.

'Have you got that newspaper with Matt's double in it?' she demanded of her astounded neighbour.

Gary kept all his discarded newspapers in a neat pile for collection by a paper-recycling company. They were, moreover, in chronological order. He took her into his garage, glancing often at her wild, uncombed hair and the V of her blouse which she hadn't, for once, buttoned to the top. 'You look different today,' he ventured.

The newspaper with the photo was missing. 'Are you sure?' she cried, ignoring Gary's pained expression as she scrabbled at the neat pile.

'Must have used it to wrap the scraps,' Gary apologised, tucking a bunch of beetroot under her arm as she left.

Darcie whirled to face him. 'How many Christopher Reynoldses would you say there were in a place the size of Sydney? Hundreds? Thousands? There must be thousands, don't you think?'

Gary's face cleared. He snapped his fingers. '*That's* the name—Reynolds! Chris Reynolds. Had a spill in some kind of car race. Looked the spitting image of Matt——'

Darcie groaned and ran home. It was probably too late to catch Matt before he parked his bike and disappeared into the rabbit-warren of the college grounds. That was, if he was really going to college. The thought was a physical blow. But there was someone who could tell her if Chris Reynolds was an alias for Matt Brooke.

Darcie spent no time hesitating at the garage door, no time girding herself to get into the Toyota. She made the journey to Ensigns in record time, screeched to a halt in the car park and headed for the upward bound lifts. It was only then that she realised she'd brought her cap. Scowling, she jammed it on her head. 'Let him be there,' she muttered.

He *was* there, seated at a desk too small for him, squeezed into a chair too narrow. Mark had made sure his nephew was not made too comfortable. Stafford swung around at the interruption.

'What is it?' he said. But then he recognised her, and his head tilted back and his eyes narrowed. Darcie gave the door a push and it half closed on his hovering, affronted secretary.

Patrick Stafford eased himself from his chair and walked over to her. Hands on hips, he studied her unbuttoned blouse, her rolled-up sleeves, her hair bunching out in sun-streaked brown waves beneath the cap.

'What happened?' he mocked, fixing on her untamed hair. 'Electric shock?'

'Chris Reynolds,' she said jerkily. 'What does he look like?'

His eyes opened wide, even the drooping left one. 'Can I have that again?'

'Christopher Reynolds,' she repeated, impatient for an answer, fearful that it would be the wrong one. She grasped Stafford's arm, giving it a small shake. He looked down rather curiously at her hand on his sleeve. 'Is he blond or dark? Is he tall or short? Is he good-looking or is he——?'

'What are you—some kind of racing groupie? I thought it was antiques you fancied.'

'Is his real name Matt Brooke?'

His eyes narrowed suspiciously. 'Now how the hell did you know that?'

It was as powerful as a blow to the solar plexus. She'd known it had to be true. Of course it had to be true. Chris Reynolds, alias Matt Brooke. But some stubborn part of her had hoped wildly that it might not be so. Blindly, Darcie turned towards the door. Matt, racing! The very thing she'd vowed would never happen. She had to go somewhere quiet and think. Patrick Stafford, however, had other ideas. He grasped her wrist and hauled her back.

'Running to Uncle with that bit of news like you did about the Rolls?' He gave her a faint, contemptuous shake. 'What I want to know is, how did you find out that the Reynolds kid is Gavin Brooke's son?'

Darcie stared at his left shoulder. Big, sloping and tense, it dragged at the fabric of his shirt, so that she could see all the separate stitches along the armhole seam. She had an insane wish to lay her head on that shoulder and weep. This piece of mental treachery jerked her out of her withdrawal, sent the blood rushing to her head in sudden fury.

'Gavin Brooke's son!' she hissed. 'That's what matters, isn't it? The son of the champion who died on the track—never mind if he has the expertise, he has the name. And, wow! Who knows, he might follow in Dad's footsteps and kill himself in front of a capacity crowd one day, which means he'll get good coverage, because who would want to miss out on a treat like that? And meanwhile, your logo spins around the track with him——'

'What the *hell* are you raving about?'

'. . . great advertising, provided of course that he doesn't kill himself *too* soon. Well, I've got news for you, you vulture. You *won't* use Matt Brooke to sell your lousy gym-bags, so forget it!' She shoved the flat of her hand against the tempting left shoulder and, astonished, he rocked at the impact. 'Take my advice, stick to football teams.'

'Football teams? *Your* advice?' he growled in crescendo. 'You're a bloody *chauffeur*, and not even a good one. No wonder the company's going down the drain. Have you been *advising* my uncle, perhaps?'

'Mark won't let you make any sponsorship offers to Matt Brooke,' she said confidently, 'when I tell him——'

That touched a raw nerve. Patrick Stafford wrapped his oversized hands around her arms and practically lifted her on to her toes. 'Tell him what you damned well like. If he can make anything out of this incoherent outburst, he's a bloody marvel—but I will do what I think best for the survival of this dinosaur of a company, and I'll stand no meddling from outside, least of all from my uncle's fancy-piece. Got that?'

Darcie took a swing at him. A straight-armed, awkward swing that probably would have gone wide of the mark even had he not blocked it. Her elbow slapped into his palm with enough force to jar her. Her cap fell off and her hair flopped over her forehead. Stafford was momentarily distracted by it. 'You tried to *hit* me!' he said, astounded, keeping a firm, close grip on her lest she try it again. He stared into her face, reviewing the features one by one as if he'd never seen them till now. 'No woman has ever tried to hit me before,' he said, his eyes lingering a moment longer on her mouth.

'Sheer luck!' she snapped.

Without releasing her, he scooped up her chauffeur's cap, then headed for the door with her in tow. 'I should fire you on the spot,' he said as they emerged into the apprehensive hush of the outer office where Mark's secretary and two juniors clustered around the computer terminal. They looked scandalised as he carted Darcie past, her feet scarcely touching the floor, like a wanted criminal being hustled into custody. Stafford ignored them. Darcie gave a grimace of pain and said, 'You're hurting my arm!' and the secretaries looked even more scandalised.

'Stop playing to the gallery,' he grunted, and roughly steered her into Mark's office.

His uncle rose slowly from his Empire pedestal desk as Stafford dumped a dishevelled Darcie on to a visitor's chair. She jumped up immediately, but Stafford leaned a hand on her shoulder and kept her there while he informed Mark that his girlfriend was a lousy chauffeur, an ineffective and unnecessary spy, and in need of psychological guidance.

'Your maladjusted mistress has been making a nuisance of herself in my office, making wild claims and accusations over the Reynolds kid, with whom I've had no more than preliminary discussions about a racing sponsorship. No doubt your loyal secretary has cut the piece out of the morning paper for you, as it mentions my name and Ensigns?'

Mark rather stiffly said he'd seen the piece. 'Is that why you're so upset, Darcie? Because Ensigns appears to be getting involved with motor racing? An ill-conceived idea as far as I am concerned . . .'

Darcie leaned forward to tell Mark just why she was so upset, but Stafford clamped her back in her seat and spoke over her.

'It may be the best piece of promotion Ensigns has ever had, because what that newshound didn't find out was that the Reynolds kid is really Gavin Brooke's son——'

He broke off at Mark's sharp reaction.

Bleakly, Darcie said, 'He used his friend's driver's licence. Chris Reynolds.'

'Matt—racing? Oh, my dear, I *am* sorry.'

Stafford looked from his uncle to Darcie. 'Do I take it you both know the boy?'

Mark steepled his fingers and looked just a fraction smug that his know-it-all nephew was caught without the full facts.

'Darcie is Matt's stepmother and guardian—a fact you would have known, Patrick, had you bothered to discuss this business with me.'

'Stepmother? Mrs Brooke? You let me think your last name was Darcy.' His gaze went to her ringless left hand, then shot upwards again as he made the computations. 'Darcie Brooke—then you must be——'

'Darcie Miller,' Mark interposed with the air of a maestro announcing a surprise guest artist. '*The* Darcie Miller.'

Patrick spun her chair on its swivel base so that she faced him. In other circumstances it would have been funny. Clearly he was having trouble reconciling this new image of a professional racing driver with her jerking starts and stops, her lousy cornering in the Rolls. 'Darcie Miller,' he said. 'Whatever happened to you?'

'Brooke,' she corrected, averting her face.

Patrick's attention intensified, and didn't waver as his uncle went on to sketch in a few details of Darcie's former career, and her marriage to Gavin.

'I've known Darcie since she was a teenager. We are just good friends, I assure you. Your wild references to girlfriends and—er—"maladjusted mistresses" are really quite ridiculous. You seem to have jumped to conclusions, Patrick,' he said with a supercilious smile that infuriated Darcie. She shot to her feet, and this time Patrick didn't stop her.

'He might have jumped to conclusions, but *you* never bothered to put it right, did you, Mark?' she snapped, to the older man's surprise. 'You deliberately didn't tell him, hoping he would make a fool of himself. Well, I hardly know him, but I can tell you that you won't stop your nephew changing things with childish games like that!'

Mark's pale cheeks flushed. He looked almost comically hurt. Patrick laughed, and Darcie turned on him.

'And *you*—I'm fed up with your sarcastic remarks about Mark's taste and appearance, as if that's all there is to him. You might be family, but you don't know the first thing about him—you haven't bothered to find out. You've come here with a head full of terrific ideas and the assumption that it has to be a battle to the death to get them accepted! It's like watching two stupid schoolboys. Why don't you both grow up?'

She snatched her cap from Stafford's hand and went to the door, buoyed up by a new anger. The two men looked at each other, then at her, and she glared back. 'I want any offer Ensigns made to Matt withdrawn at once. There! Now you have something *new* to squabble about!'

CHAPTER THREE

THE STREET Darcie lived in could be the set of a movie, Patrick thought. Modest post-war houses, trimmed hedges, neat flowerbeds, letter-boxes all in a row. Sprinklers sprayed, lawn-mowers revved, dogs barked. A gang of children rode trikes and bicycles on the footpath. Time: a Sunday afternoon, late summer. Place: typical suburbia.

Now what, he asked himself as he spotted Darcie's house number, was a former professional driver, accustomed to an international life-style, doing in a nice, average place like this?

She was in the driveway, washing her car, and didn't hear him pull up. Patrick made his way in through a small gate and stood for a moment, looking around at her garden. Roses everywhere. The fragrance was really something. There were beds full of flowering bushes, and ramblers trailing over trellises, and a climbing rose covered in white flowers framed the front veranda entrance. A rose-covered cottage, he thought, and frowned at the cliché. He went across the lawn to Darcie, who was still unaware of his presence. She was barefoot, wearing shorts and a T-shirt, and was on tiptoe, swirling suds on to the roof of her Toyota with a sponge.

Patrick eyed her legs with interest. Very nice. Her uniform didn't do her justice. Her backside jiggled from side to side as she rubbed at a mark on the car and, as she stretched further, her shorts pulled up to reveal the pale lower swell of her buttocks. Smiling, he delayed announcing himself for a minute or two and appreciated this new view of his chauffeur. Eventually he said, 'You really do grow roses.'

Darcie whirled around, her hand tightening on the king-sized sponge she held. White foam bubbled from it.

'What are you doing here?' she demanded, transferring bits of froth to her forehead as she swept back some damp strands of hair.

'How long would it take you to dress?' he asked, keeping a wary eye on the sponge.

'I'm not going anywhere.'

'A short drive, I thought,' he said. 'We could talk about Matt.'

She turned her back, slapped the sponge on to the Toyota's bonnet, and flecks of foam flew. Patrick wiped one from the lens of his sunglasses.

'No, thanks. I discussed Matt with Mark yesterday, as he *is* still running Ensigns, and I have his assurance that there will be no sponsorship.'

Patrick's temper frayed around the edges. 'Things change, even in a mausoleum like Ensigns. Mark might not be in any position to deliver such a promise. Maybe you should hedge your bets, Darcie.'

'If you had the clout, you would have taken over by now.'

'I have the clout,' he assured her. 'You can choose not to believe me, but why risk it?'

Mutinously, she dumped half a bucket of sudsy water on the car's rear. 'If you want to talk about Matt, you can talk here.'

'Doesn't suit me, not with your neighbour across the road watching us like a hawk.' He glanced over at the man who was keeping surveillance as he mowed his lawn. 'Of course, he might just be ogling your legs.' He did some more ogling himself, and earned a Valkyrian glare. She looked ferocious, yet oddly fragile, at one and the same time. Knowing who she was, Patrick found it intriguing. 'You can't force me to turn Matt down, you know. But you might persuade me.'

Her eyes flashed contemptuously. 'Oh, *persuade*, is it?'

'Yes, my pretty,' he leered. 'Let me have my wicked way with you, or you'll be sorry! Come on, act your age, Darcie,' he said, suddenly not so amused at her implication. 'So far all I've had is hysterics from you and obstruction from Mark. You want a concession from me, OK. I don't negotiate with unreasonable women who take punches at me. Talk to me, give me your view, explain yourself. Is fifteen minutes long enough for you to change?' He looked at her dirty bare feet, her lovely suds-smeared legs, her birds-nest hair, and smiled. 'Better make it half an hour.'

It was intended as a challenge, to make her prove she could be ready sooner rather than later, so Darcie took the full thirty minutes. Let him wait. She showered, towelled off, then surveyed herself seriously in the misted mirror. 'You might persuade me' he'd said. Maybe she *should* try some persuasion, at that. She shook out her hair and studied the result. Some extra eye make-up perhaps, some of that bronze blusher that she hadn't used in an age, a squirt of French perfume, a dress that showed off her legs. He seemed to like her legs. It pleased her, brought a gleam to her eyes.

In her bedroom, she peeked through the curtain and saw him standing in the front garden beside a rose-bed. As she watched he casually caught hold of a full-blown pink rose, its petals ready to fall, and bent over it, presumably to sniff its fragrance. Darcie let the curtain fall into place and turned away. Poor rose, she thought, imagining his big hand clutching it. Only seconds from extinction. Any tentative notions of playing up to him died stone-dead. Stafford wasn't the kind of man to be swayed by winsome smiles and flattery, and she wasn't the kind of woman to turn it on.

Briskly, she dressed in grey twill trousers and a pastel pink shirt and low shoes, subjugated her hair into a neat twist, and used some lipstick. But that earlier train of thought made her reach for her French perfume. When she sprayed, only air puffed on to her neck. She peered into the crystal perfume vial. Nothing there but a line of dark gold around the base. Her favourite perfume must have evaporated away, dried up ages ago, and she hadn't noticed.

Stafford held the front passenger door open for her. It was an odd reversal of their relationship, and Darcie viewed it with distrust. Much better the way things had been—she at the Rolls's wheel, he tending his paperwork in the back, and the partition in between. She had a sudden, poignant longing for that partition.

He gave her the once-over and smiled sardonically. 'Back in camouflage gear, I see.'

'I don't know what you mean.'

' "Mrs Suburban Housewife",' he drawled. 'You should get rid of those shorts. They're out of character.'

'What are you talking about?'

He just smiled, shut the door, and went around to the driver's side. 'You won't be too critical, I hope,' he said as he started the car. And when she looked at him in perplexity, he went on, 'Of my driving. I feel rather inadequate.'

She couldn't hold back a hoot of laughter. 'Inadequate? Do you *ever* feel inadequate?'

'I've never driven a professional driver before.'

'Ex-professional,' she said, all amusement fleeing. 'It doesn't mean anything any more.'

'You made it in one of the toughest fields. A male-dominated one, at that. It means you must have guts and dedication and will-power, as well as talent. I have to admit, I'm impressed.'

Darcie glanced at him, startled. There was sincerity in his tone, and admiration. Hard-to-please Patrick Stafford admired her! Well, dammit, she didn't want his admiration or anyone else's, had avoided it like the plague for years—but even as she rejected it, she experienced a fleeting pleasure.

'I thought the object of this "short drive" was to discuss Matt,' she said stonily.

'You weren't tempted to go back to driving when you were widowed?' He went on as if she hadn't spoken.

'No. I wasn't.'

'Lost your nerve when your husband was killed?'

'Anyone with any sensitivity wouldn't ask a question like that.'

'The ex-pro driver who carried off a Touring Car Classic first, made it into the top three at Bathurst, and still holds a practice lap record at Lakeside, gets nervous driving a Rolls around city streets. I think it's a fair question.'

'How do you know all that?'

'It's all in the files.'

She swallowed. 'Files?'

'Newspaper files. I've put together a nice little dossier on Darcie Miller.' He tossed her a glance, mimicked a newsboy's call, 'Reading all about you.'

Not *all* about her, she thought. Not everything was in the files. 'Ancient history,' she said shortly.

' "In our past lies our present." I'm misquoting someone, but you know what I mean.'

It made her feel extraordinarily vulnerable. But, she reminded herself, as Matt's guardian she came under the heading of a potential business deal to this man. He was merely doing his research.

'You'll have read in the files that I retired when I married Gavin. There isn't room in a marriage for two professional drivers, so I gave it up. After he was killed, I didn't want anything to do with racing. I don't like driving at all now, if you must know, but, as Gavin's manager robbed him blind and left us with precious little after the debts were paid, I need a job, so I force myself. Does that satisfy you?'

'Nope,' he said, 'but it will have to do for now. What do you call that pink rose-bush?'

'What pink rose-bush?' she asked, confounded by the sudden switch.

'The one I was looking at when you were playing peekaboo at the window.'

'I was not——' she denied, and stopped in annoyance. The man was extraordinarily observant. Uncomfortably, she filed the information away. 'It's called a Princess Margaret rose. Why?'

'I like it. Might buy a couple of bushes. Can you

recommend any others?'

'You want to buy rose-bushes?'

'For my garden. Will they grow in tubs?'

He was, he told her, renovating a place he'd bought as an investment years ago before he'd gone overseas.

'It was built originally as a warehouse. I got it cheap because it was in such a mess and close to a railway line.'

'Doesn't the noise bother you?'

'No. I like the sound of trains. Always was crazy about trains as a kid. We didn't, of course, ever live near anything so plebeian as a railway line. My parents wouldn't like my place at all.'

Any parents would have reservations about a run-down warehouse beside a railway line, she thought, and Patrick's parents moved in Melbourne society's exclusive circles.

'But that only makes it more attractive, doesn't it?' she said, making a shrewd guess.

He seemed startled. 'What makes you say that?'

'From what I can see, you like to shock your family. Aren't you a little old to be a rebel still?'

He gave a huff of laughter. 'In my family, you conform or you rebel. I never had it in me to conform.'

'It can't have been as bad as that——' she began, when she realised that the road he was following was a very familiar one. 'Where is this "short drive" taking us?' she asked, lightly enough, for the road, after all, led to other places. Stafford's swift glance gave her the answer. Her heart thudded.

'Oh, no! No,' she said tautly, 'take me home.'

'The subject for discussion is Matt. And you've never even seen him race.'

See him race? Adrenalin pounded through her veins.

She felt sick, physically sick. 'I don't want to see him race. Stop the car——'

'Look,' he said in a reasonable tone, 'I understand that it's hard for you, after what happened to your husband, but you have to see him drive some time.'

As the traffic slowed she made a grab for the door-handle, but Stafford was quicker. There was a clunk as he switched on the central-locking system. The door wouldn't budge. 'You pig!' she hissed, rattling the handle. 'Let me out. I feel sick,' she added, warningly.

'There are some tissues in the glove compartment,' he said, unmoved by the threat that she might throw up on his upholstery, 'but I don't think you'll be sick, somehow.'

'I won't go in. I won't watch.'

'Please yourself. But I'm not turning back, so you can cut the dramatics.'

The car joined the racetrack queue, and moved through the gates to the car park. The moment he unlocked the doors, Darcie was out, with every intention of sprinting for the nearest exit. But the sound stopped her—the sound of cars in contest. A distant drone that swelled to a growl, then a snarling roar, and the whoosh as the air rocked at the passing of tonnes of steel. And there was the racetrack smell, as sharply familiar as if she'd never been away. Oil and fuel, exhaust fumes and overheated rubber. It was a flavour, a taste almost, sweet and bitter in her mouth and nostrils.

When Stafford took her arm she went unresisting, bombarded by the emotions the place evoked. Joy, triumph, desolation, pain. Fear. By the time he had guided her on to grass, among scattered spectators, she was rigid with fear. The last time she'd stood like this at a racetrack, someone she'd loved had died.

The current race had two laps to go. Darcie didn't look at the track. She looked around at the crowd and wondered how many of them had watched Gavin's crash on television. Ordinary looking people—gawky teenage boys and middle-aged husbands and wives and pretty girls showing off in designer pit-suits and boots. Small children who had to be lifted to see what was happening. Perspiration misted her brow and, shakily, she wiped it away with the tips of her fingers. One of the middle-aged wives stared at her, and Darcie thought she must look as pale as she felt.

The winner streaked home to applause. That, too, was a sharp, familiar memory that part of her suddenly responded to, yearned for again, and part of her loathed.

'Bad, is it?' Stafford said, beside her. He looked down at her with academic interest, not sympathy, and it resuscitated her anger.

'You'll never know,' she hissed, '*or* care.'

He made no reply, but presently, when the next race was called and the cars moved into starting positions, he put his arm around her shoulders. 'Matt's number eight,' he said, ignoring her attempt to turn aside. That was what the bracing arm was for, she thought bitterly—not to comfort, but to enforce.

She tried not to watch, tried hard. But her eyes strayed to the crouching pack of cars as the guttural revving of motors reached a crescendo, and when the race started she followed number eight. Not a good start. 'Too much clutch——' she muttered. She would tell him that what he should do was . . . She felt Stafford's eyes on her, and stopped. Of course she wouldn't. Advising Matt on how to most efficiently go and kill himself was exactly what she would *never* do. Her brow was slick with perspiration now, her mind offering up silent prayers for Matt's safety, making silent vows to separate him from this insane sport that had been her life. Yet a small, repressed part of her functioned independently, critically, noting the strengths and the flaws in his car and his performance.

He finished third.

'I thought he might finish better than that,' Stafford said.

'He finished alive,' she said, pleased that he seemed disappointed in Matt's driving. 'That's all that interests me. That and making sure he gives it up.'

'Still, for his age and experience he shows some skill.'

'He shows very little skill,' she said flatly. 'Matt has raw talent and good instincts, but no discipline. He's all adolescent gung-ho. What he needs is to sharpen up his——' She bit her lip. 'What he needs is to stop wasting his time and concentrate on his studies.'

'I don't think he's going to do that, somehow.' He smiled and she followed his gaze to see Matt being kissed enthusiastically by one of the pretty, long-legged race groupies.

'That's the glamorous side of it when you're a kid. Not many make it past the ego-trip. It's too much hard work. When they find out what a grind it is, and how hard it is to get decent backers, they fold up,' she said, but she looked at Matt, so at home, so at ease on the track, and so much better a driver than she was admitting, and she was afraid. 'Can we go now? I don't want Matt to see me.'

'Hmm.' Stafford looked thoughtful. 'Always supposing he made it past the glamour, he's still raw.

What he needs is a stint at a decent racing school and a couple of years of hard work, and even then he might not prove a winner.'

Darcie found this very hopeful. She had not, she saw now, been taking the right tack with Stafford. He was profit-orientated and saw the entire business in terms of returns on his investment. Her problem was that she was too emotionally involved, and emotion was clearly not the way to influence this man. 'Why throw your money away on a novice,' she said, forcing herself to clear her mind, 'when there are established drivers winning races, drawing crowds, just crying out for sponsorship?' As they made their way through the crowd she laid out for him unemotionally the kind of exposure Ensigns could expect from an established driver with a back-up team. 'Of course, you should seriously consider whether motor racing will offer you any measurable return in terms of promotion. It makes sense for the auto spare-parts people and cigarette and beer producers to sponsor racing, but leathergoods? I'm not so sure.'

'Would it sell gym-bags, you mean?' he murmured, a humorous light in his eyes. Or his left eye, at any rate.

'A football team might give you better exposure.'

'Or a golfer.'

'A golfer would be ideal,' she said too quickly.

He smiled again and took her arm. 'You could be right.'

A sigh escaped Darcie. This afternoon's trauma was all worthwhile if it discouraged Stafford, who in turn would discourage Matt. All the same, she quickened her stride, anxious to leave the racetrack.

'Excuse me,' a breathless voice said behind her, just

before they emerged into the car park. It was the middle-aged woman who had stared at her earlier. 'Aren't you Darcie Miller?' She had a race programme and a pen tentatively poised, and Darcie took both without thinking and signed her name. She stood there staring at her signature while the woman apologised for not recognising her sooner. 'Are you making a comeback, Darcie? I wish you would. Oh, thanks for this!'

Darcie released the pen and programme into her hands and stared after her as she hurried away.

'It must be like riding a bike,' Patrick said, shrewdly observing her confusion. 'You never forget.'

It had been such a long time. As a driver she was ancient history, yet after a few hours at a racetrack she had responded to an autograph-hunter as if she'd never been away. She'd signed the programme without a moment's hesitation—Darcie *Miller*. The treacherous thought occurred to her—would all her other reflexes still be as ingrained? She set her jaw and stared out of the window. She would never know the answer to that.

He dropped her at her house. 'Goodbye,' he said. 'It's been illuminating.'

Illuminating! He'd flayed her to the bone, exposed her fear and her weaknesses, and he called it illuminating. The man had about as much sensitivity as a rhinoceros. Though why malign a rhinoceros? she thought. On her way inside she passed the pink rose he'd been sniffing at earlier. Beautiful, overblown, but still intact, it swayed a little on its long stem. She gave a smile, remembering the way he had carelessly caught hold of it. No finesse at all. Only the sturdiest of roses could survive.

'Congratulations, Princess,' she said wryly under her breath, and reached out to it. At the merest touch of her fingertip it fell apart.

Matt came home that evening and told her a pack of lies about the weekend he'd spent studying at Chris's place. The temptation to tell him she knew the truth was great, but she resisted it. She would wait until Stafford burst his bubble and see what happened. Matt, convinced that the son of Gavin Brooke would be snapped up by a sponsor, might lose interest when he found it wasn't so. And then too, if she waited, Matt might confide in her. Surely, in his disappointment he would come to her? That became steadily more important to Darcie.

She was not required to drive Patrick Stafford at all on Monday, nor on Tuesday. Matt's moods continued to swing wildly between elation and guilt, she thought, recalling derisively that she had imagined him in love. His bubble didn't burst or, if it did, she saw no sign of it. Darcie's appetite dried up, she lost sleep, and when she did sleep she had the dream.

On Wednesday she drove Stafford again. He was turned out in the beige trousers and tweedy sports jacket. There were blade-like creases in the trousers now, and his shirt was creaseless, which meant, she supposed, that he had found another housekeeper. Poor thing, catering to Patrick's needs in a partly renovated warehouse. She must have been desperate for work.

He looked her over with a reminiscent smile. 'I liked the shorts better,' he told her as he got into the car.

'Have you spoken to Matt yet?' she asked, in no mood for reminders of Sunday.

Yes, he had spoken to Matt.

'When was that?'

Monday. 'Monday?' she repeated, feeling a rush of

warmth to her face. All that wondering and waiting and all for nothing. 'Why didn't you tell me?'

'Why didn't Matt?'

It was an unerring strike at her weakest point. In the rear-view mirror he met her eyes levelly with that same academic interest and lack of sympathy that infuriated her. As a mother figure she was a failure, he seemed to be saying, and was mildly curious to see how she took it.

'He didn't seem very—disappointed,' she said, swallowing down her resentment.

'That's because I didn't exactly turn him down.'

The Rolls lurched as her hands jerked on the wheel, the tyres squealed as she overcorrected. 'But I thought you were going to look for a football team, or a golfer——'

'This is obviously not the time to discuss it,' he said drily, recovering his papers which had fanned out across the back seat. 'Anyway, I'm up to my ears in work. Why don't I come to your place tonight, and we'll talk then?'

Casually he slammed the partition shut. Darcie reached around and slammed it open again.

'It might not suit me to have you calling at my place tonight. In fact, it *doesn't* suit me.'

'Your mud-wrestling night?' he enquired, dead-pan.

That he could be humorous at a time like this only fanned her anger.

'Tell me now what you told Matt,' she demanded.

'Not while you're driving. I have very powerful survival instincts.' He closed the partition.

Darcie opened it again.

'All right, I'll stop the car and you can tell me.'

'You'll do what you're paid to do, and drive.'

Darcie cast a louring look at his reflection in the

mirror. Dictatorial creep. It wouldn't hurt him to stop for a few minutes to put her out of her misery. Short of kidnapping the man and forcing him to talk, there was nothing for it but to wait until tonight. Kidnapping. She let the word and the idea turn over a few times. She was in control of the car, wasn't she? And he was more or less captive in the back. Well, then . . . Darcie squared her ethical arguments with the reminder that, after Sunday, it was poetic justice. A few minutes later she altered her course. Stafford, frowning over a wad of notes, didn't notice. Even when the Lane Cove River came into sight, her passenger didn't look up. He didn't do that until the Rolls bumped into a riverside reserve.

She stopped the car, removed the keys from the ignition and the spares from the glove compartment, and went around to Stafford's door. It jerked open and an incredulous Patrick Stafford emerged. Shoulders hunched, he would have made a great head-piece for an ancient battering ram.

'What the hell are we doing in a children's playground?' he asked, spreading his hands to indicate the swings and the see-saws and the roundabout.

'What do you mean, you didn't *exactly* turn Matt down?' Darcie said doggedly.

Stafford stared. 'Am I to understand that you're on strike?'

'You agreed he was raw and you'd be better off with a golfer, so why haven't you told him you're not interested?'

He set his hands on his hips—an intimidating move if ever there was one. It extended an already impressive shoulderline and swelled his chest until a line of key-holes opened up between all the buttons of his shirt,

small showcases for dark, curling chest hair. 'Why me?'
he addressed the sky above. 'Why did *I* have to get the
dizzy woman driver with a past? Hell—you seemed
normal enough at first,' he accused. 'Next thing you're
canoodling on the couch with Uncle, then careering
around my office throwing punches, *then* you're
unveiled as a former racing driver with a stepson who
turns out to be the dead pushy kid who elbowed his way
in to see me about sponsoring him! It's like a bloody
soap opera that goes on and on—I think Mark gave me
you on purpose. Piling on the pressure to make me
crack.' He shook his head in exasperation. 'To think I
came close to taking you out—a quiet, relaxing dinner
somewhere, I thought, dancing maybe.' He gave a hoot
of derision. 'What a disaster that would have been!'

'There was no question of disaster because I said no, if
you remember,' she said hotly.

He waved a hand in an arrogant, throw-away gesture.
'I could have changed your mind if I'd worked on it.'

Darcie's mouth dropped open. 'You—ignorant,
conceited pig! You're one of those primitives who still
believes that a woman can't say no and mean it. Well, let
me tell you——'

He cast his eyes upwards again. 'Spare me the
histrionics. I have enough on my hands just trying to
drag my uncle and the board screaming into the
twentieth century. Right now, I could do without any
extra drama. What I need is a nice, quiet, efficient driver
who gives me no hassles, and a nice, warm, stable
woman who is passionate about something other than
her domestic life.'

'In other words you're looking for a nice doormat that
says "welcome"!' she sneered. 'If you're so dissatisfied

with me, why haven't you requested another driver?'

He tilted his head to one side and looked her over. 'All the others have hairy legs,' he said reflectively.

Darcie gave a snort of annoyance. 'I want to know what you told Matt,' she said with a firmness she didn't feel. She felt rather light-headed out here in the sun. Not enough sleep, no breakfast, and Patrick Stafford—a combination guaranteed to make anyone light-headed.

'I told you—we'll discuss it tonight.' He checked his watch and scowled. 'I'm late already for my appointment, so cut this nonsense and drive me to Chatswood, or I'll remove those keys from you forcibly and drive myself.'

He waited a moment, then stepped towards her, reaching confidently for the keys. Darcie sprang back, yanked the top two buttons of her blouse open, and dropped the Rolls key-ring into the left cup of her bra, the spares into the right.

'We'll stay here until you talk to me,' she told him, conscious that the ultimatum lost a little of its dramatic value as she twitched to dislodge the cold, sharp edge of a key cutting into her left breast.

A long pause. Darcie rotated her shoulder in an unobtrusive effort to coax the key downwards. Stafford leaned back against the Rolls, crossed one foot in front of the other, and watched.

'I don't know whether to be flattered or insulted . . .' he said.

Darcie flexed her ribcage. The key stayed painfully in place.

'. . . that you think those are safe in there.' His eyes steadied on her blouse front. 'The keys, I mean,' he added sardonically, pausing to let her get his meaning.

'Either you think I'm a perfect gentleman, or that I'm intimidated by the idea of rummaging in an occupied bra.'

She flushed. Rummaging in an occupied bra? She took a look at his large, capable hands and his long, long reach, and backed off a pace. If it came to it, could she make it into the Rolls before he caught her? He grinned nastily as she measured the distance in quick little glances.

'I'll give you a ten-second start if you like,' he offered.

'Oh, this isn't a joking matter! You said—you indicated that a golfer would suit you better——'

'I changed my mind.'

'But why?'

'I'm a masochist,' he sneered. 'I found a pushy seventeen-year-old kid and his avenging stepmama just too good to pass up!'

Unsteadily, she put up a hand to shade her eyes. The movement seemed to irritate him.

'Playing to the gallery again? Forget it—I'm too old to fall for the tragedy queen act.'

'What?' she asked, puzzled.

'Look—I talked to the kid again and I was impressed. He seems determined to race, determined enough to go behind your back and risk your wrath. Somehow or other he intends to get some finance. He told me he wants to be the best, like his father.'

Darcie swayed, put out a hand for support, but no support was there. 'It's just a phase he's going through,' she said desperately. 'Nearly every boy wants to be a racing driver, or an astronaut, or a—a pop star. He bought an electric guitar, learned some chords, formed a band and lost interest in it, all within four months last year. And he'll lose interest in racing if he's just left alone——'

'And what will you do if he doesn't? He'll be eighteen soon, and legally entitled to make any deals he can for himself. The sooner you face the fact, the sooner you can do something sensible about protecting him. Or would you prefer to bury your head in the sand while the kid makes disastrous decisions about his future?'

The strain of the past three years was tight around her chest, compressing her breath. 'You haven't got a sympathetic bone in your body, have you?'

'It isn't sympathy you need,' he said. 'From what I can see, people have been tiptoeing around you for years, letting you camouflage yourself in some fairy-tale world of rose-covered cottages and safe suburbia. Did you really think a kid with Matt's background would be satisfied with roses and a nine-to-five future? Or are you too damned selfish to care?'

'Selfish? You *dare* to say that——'

'The kid is in agony wondering how he's going to tell you he wants the very thing you hate. He's burning up with guilt and every time he manages to get it under control, I gather, you very conveniently wake up in a tizzy, screaming at a nightmare, and he feels like a louse all over again. It's been three years. Isn't it time the nightmares stopped, whether they're genuine or not?'

'Genuine?' she croaked, feeling bruised. 'What are you saying?'

'I'm saying that it's dead easy to manipulate a kid who's torn between what he wants and a desire to protect you.'

The blood rushed from Darcie's head. 'You don't know anything . . . I wish they *weren't* genuine. I wish they'd stop. I'd never use a thing like that to upset Matt. I try to *hide* them from him, damn you!' Her voice broke, and Stafford blinked a bit, frowning.

'You've got the experience to help Matt,' he said in a softer tone. 'Stop trying to pretend that you're a suburban housewife with a son who's going to be an accountant. You're a former racing driver. And Matt's a future one.'

'No. *No!*' The peaceful parkland undulated. Darcie closed her eyes. 'Not Matt too—I couldn't bear it . . .' There was a buzzing in her ears and she knew she was falling, and there was the support she'd sought, an arm around her waist. She was held close to a warm, strong body that smelled so nice, so masculine and musky. She felt a sharp pain in her breast before everything turned dark.

CHAPTER FOUR

THE rocking motion woke her, puzzled her. Where was she? Then she heard her name said softly—'Darcie'—and, eyes closed, she smiled. She was cradled in gentle arms and the world swayed sweetly beneath her, so of course she had to be on the boat, Gavin's boat that he'd bought so impulsively, blowing his Monza prize money on it. *Darling Darcie,* he'd named her. They were in the Aegean now, between islands, the three of them brown and as near naked as they could be. Gavin, raven-haired and godlike, and twelve-year-old Matt, skinny in briefest togs, herself in a string bikini. The boat's rigging creaked lazily. The water was so calm today, just an occasional peaceful swell. Matt was stretched out asleep in the sun, which meant that she and Gavin could go below . . . she half opened her eyes. The sky was a glorious Grecian blue. Smiling, she hooked her arm around his neck, twined her fingers in his hair.

'I want to make love, Gavin, darling,' she murmured. The sun blazed down from above him, hazing his image into a silhouette as she pulled his head down to her.

'Darcie——' he said, and his voice was odd, rougher than usual. 'I'm not——' He was teasing, pretending to be reluctant. Darcie smiled, linked her arms around his neck and kissed him, moving her mouth provocatively on his, flicking her tongue along his lower lip and laugh-

60

ing as he remained aloof. Then, gradually, he surrendered, his mouth became mobile, parted, and something was different, very different, yet good. Before she could properly sample the difference, he withdrew, and she felt her wrists gripped and her arms firmly disengaged from about his neck.

'Darcie.'

This time she recognised the rough timbre of the voice. She woke fully and squinted up at the sky. Not the clear, soft Greek light, but uncompromising Australian. He leaned over her and blocked the sun's glare, and she stared at the face that came into focus. Not handsome brown eyes and curling black hair and smooth-textured olive skin, but lopsided grey and coarse, straight brown and grainy, light tan. Not Gavin's gentle arms and the swell of the Aegean, but Patrick Stafford holding her on his lap and the faint, creaking motion of the roundabout upon which he sat with her. Her eyes wandered up the thin metal struts attached to the roundabout's central pole. A mast and boat's rigging, she had thought, in that foolish moment of disorientation.

Patrick Stafford. She'd kissed him.

'Oh! I—er——' she said huskily as she lay back in his arms, looking at him. He wore the oddest expression. One that she'd never seen before on either side of his face. She'd *kissed* him. Run her hands through his hair. The enormity of it pushed out the pang of regret that Gavin and childishly skinny Matt and the *Darling Darcie* were all just tricks of memory, illusions. Even now, knowing it was him she'd kissed, the languid, pleasant sensation lingered. She must be mad.

'What happened?' she asked, as if she didn't remember a thing. He wasn't fooled by it, she could see. But, after a momentary hesitation, he merely said, 'You passed out.'

'Oh.' A moment longer she stayed there, as if it was perfectly natural to be held across his knee while he sat on a listing, creaking roundabout. It was peaceful, comforting even, but it couldn't last. She sat up suddenly, tears prickling at her eyelids. 'You're a former racing driver. And Matt's a future one,' he'd said, summing up all that she'd denied these past years. 'He wants to be the best, like his father.' She'd always known it could be so. Deep down she'd known, but avoided the knowledge, postponed facing it, tried to make a life excluding it, blinding herself to the clues to the contrary. Now she felt painfully stupid, like some mad Canute sitting on an empty beach trying to stop the tide.

'But I can't let it happen!' she burst out as the tears overflowed. 'I mustn't let it happen again.'

'Here.' He pressed a handkerchief into her hand, and when she just looked at it he said drily, 'It's clean.'

Incredibly, she choked back a laugh as she took it. It was finest lawn, monogrammed classically with his entwined initials—a touch of class for a man who wore budget suits and out-of-date shirts. She mopped her eyes with it.

'What do you dream?' he asked after a while.

Darcie looked at him. 'Don't you mean, what do I *pretend* to dream?'

'I'll grovel, if you like.'

The sidelong apology made her smile for a moment. Looking away towards the river, she said, 'It's always on a racetrack. I try to overtake him, because I know if I can just change the sequence of the race, he won't crash.

But—I never can, and his car always rolls and goes up in flames.'

Patrick was very still. 'Bloody hell,' he muttered, 'you blame yourself!'

'I could have stopped him racing. *Should* have stopped him. I didn't argue strongly enough. I didn't use the *right* arguments. I should have told him I'd leave him if he didn't retire.' Darcie swallowed hard on years of regret. 'He's be alive if I'd used the right arguments.'

'You think you failed him?'

'I did fail him.'

'And you think you're failing Matt if you don't stop him racing?'

His prosaic tone had a bracing effect. 'Yes,' she said, eyeing him resentfully over his damp handkerchief.

'You're flaying yourself unnecessarily. You don't have the power to arrange people's fates.'

'You wouldn't understand,' she said. 'When you love someone, you have a responsibility. When something happens to them, you feel you should have *done* something, protected them better——'

'Protect them, even against their will? Sounds more like ownership than love. You respected your husband's dreams, so you didn't use emotional blackmail to try to make him give them up. You'll have to respect Matt's dreams too, even if they lead him into danger. If you don't, you'll lose him.'

The baldly stated truth was like a knife in her ribs. Glaring at him, she leapt up, her heels wobbling on the grooved track that circled the roundabout. Only his swift support prevented her from falling.

'Take it easy,' he warned. 'Intriguing though it was, I don't want you passing out again. Sit down, will you?'

'No, thanks.' Darcie pulled against his grip, which would normally have been like tugging at the moorings of the QE2, but the roundabout, built to respond to a push from a child, began to turn. Darcie, anxious to put some distance between them, kept right on going, and Stafford, afraid to let her go because she might faint again, held on to her, so around they went. Her head spun as the roundabout creaked into high gear.

'Stop running!' he bellowed.

'You let go!' she yelled.

He said something else she didn't catch and then, unexpectedly, he was laughing, softly at first, then a full-scale belly-laugh that rang out over the empty park. Darcie stared at him as she jogged along, no longer dragging the roundabout, but being dragged by its accumulated force. The absurdity of it hit her and she began to laugh, too. Patrick chose his moment and let her go. She careered away and fell into long grass, and he came off at a run as the roundabout spun. He grasped her hand and hauled her to her feet and she came up close to him. Patrick was smiling still, not a big, definite showing of teeth, but rather a subtle shift of each feature. A smile could flash out and be withdrawn in an instant, but this soaked-in warmth looked enduring.

'What it must be like to go twenty laps with you at Bathurst,' he murmured. Then, prosaically, 'You'd better eat something before you wilt again. Have you got any food with you?'

'Sandwiches in the car.'

He pressed her down on one of the swing seats and fetched her sandwiches. 'Eat,' he directed, 'and listen.'

He strolled about for a moment while she unwrapped her sandwiches and took a half-hearted bite from one.

Then he stood squarely in front of her, stuck his hands in his pockets, and looked thoughtfully at her. The usual mix of signals reached Darcie. From the left, a speculative warmth, interest—from the right, calculation and that detached academic assessment.

'Ensigns is going into a new market area—we are looking for a new advertising image, and someone like Matt could be it.' He held up a hand resignedly as she swallowed down a chunk of sandwich to protest. 'I only say *could* be. At the moment the concept itself is still in doubt because, whatever you might think, I have no intention of ramming it down Mark's throat, and I have to prove its worth. Matt's a sponsor's dream in one way—he's young, enthusiastic, photogenic, talented, and he has the spillover glamour of being his father's son. Just *listen*!' he repeated as she tried to speak. 'In other ways he's an unknown quantity. I think you could be wrong about Matt changing his mind about racing——' his mouth twisted as if in acknowledgement of this unusual display of tact '—however, you are his stepmother and guardian, and I have to concede that there may be something in what you say . . . Can I have one of those?' He looked hopefully at her sandwiches and, taking her silence for consent, took one. 'As we're agreed that, for the moment, Matt seems bent on competing, as he doesn't turn eighteen for a few months, and as it will take at least that long for us to sort out our new product image, why don't we wait and see?' The sandwich was gone in two bites and he looked hungrily down at her remaining lunch. 'Why not relieve the pressure on Matt by bringing the whole business out into the open? That way we'll both have a chance to assess just how serious he is about racing. If it's just an

ego trip or a passing phase like the guitar——' he said it
blandly without a flicker of irony '—then nothing will
have been lost. If it isn't, you won't be able to stop him
anyway, and we'd make as good a sponsor as most.
Better.'

'How can I be sure of that?' she said, and felt the
sickly fear that comes of burning one's boats.

'We could draw up an agreement with suitable escape
clauses for both parties—as guardian you would have a
major input. And think of it this way: if Matt's tied to us
as a major sponsor, however conditionally, no one else
can make him offers that might to go his head.'

It held a lot of appeal. The only thing she would like
more would be for Matt to give up driving completely,
but already she felt the chances of that happening were
slim. Still, the arrangement kept alive some hope that by
eighteen he might have lost interest. If Stafford had
suggested a set-up that hadn't included that hope, she
would have fought him all the way. She looked at him
consideringly.

'You're much cleverer than I thought,' she said. 'Do
your family realise how clever you are?'

'I don't know. They put so much store on
appearances.' Grinning, he dabbed up the crumbs in her
lunch-wrapper with the tip of a finger. 'So do you.'

She eyed his shirt and the tweedy sports jacket, both
stretched to the limit across his shoulders. 'Don't you
care how you look?'

He laughed as if at a private joke. 'You mean clothes?
Not that much. But I'm intrigued that *you* do.' He
walked around behind her and gave the swing a push.
'All that brushing and combing and straightening my
tie. Must be some maternal instinct. Women like to

think men can't get along without their help.'

'Well, you could certainly do with some help in choosing clothes.'

'Are you volunteering?'

'No, I'm not. And stop pushing the swing.'

'Yes, maternal instinct,' he repeated aggravatingly. 'You'd probably be disappointed if I gave you a good reason for dressing the way I do.'

'If you could give me a good reason, I'd be *astonished*.'

He laughed again and gave the swing a mighty push. Darcie yelled in protest, but went up, way up, and unexpectedly her spirits soared too. The air rushed past, dragged her hair from its restraining pins, and flipped it forward as she made dizzying sweep after sweep into blue sky. The swing squeaked satisfactorily, reminding her of other swings and other times. As a child she had dared herself to leap off at the highest point of the arc, hurtling through the air to see how far away she could land. But she wasn't a child now. Darcie scuffed a foot on the ground to stop the swing. Embarrassed, a little breathless, she came back to earth, stood up, brushed crumbs from her uniform, and fixed her hair. Patrick was by the roundabout, idly pushing it. She thought for a moment that he was going to step on to the seat as it revolved, but he glanced over his shoulder, saw her looking, and walked over to her. Darcie narrowed her eyes. There was something sheepish about his sudden change of direction. She smiled, maliciously delighted. He *had* been about to take a ride on the roundabout.

He consulted his watch as he powered past her. 'Are you all right to drive? I'm late, and we're not paying you to frolic in children's playgrounds. Let's go.'

'Yes, *sir*!' She snapped out a salute that was entirely

wasted, for he was already ahead of her. When she
reached the Rolls he was leaning against it, arms crossed
over his chest and a disconcertingly quizzical look in his
eyes. It took her a moment to think why. The keys, of
course! He was going to take great pleasure in seeing her
fish down her front for the car keys.

She turned her back on him to retrieve them. She
patted left, she patted right. No keys. Must have slipped
down, she thought, patting lower. Come to think of it,
she hadn't felt that metal edge biting into her for some
time. She gave an experimental twitch, then patted all
down her front with increasing urgency. They *had* to be
here! Because if they weren't . . .

From behind her came the faint jingle of metal on
metal. She turned around, hands still spread hopefully
on her bosom. The two sets of keys dangled from one of
Stafford's large hands. Darcie turned a deep, brick-red.

Eyes gleaming with enjoyment, he tossed the keys to
her. 'Don't think about it,' he said.

But she did think about it. *Steamed* about it. So
preoccupied was she with the vivid images of her
unconscious self being manhandled, that it was hours
before she thought seriously again of Matt and what lay
ahead. Much later it occurred to her that Stafford might
have made a very sound psychological move.

She was sitting in the lounge drinking a whisky and
dry when Matt came home. That she was drinking was
unusual enough to bring a frown to his brow. Darcie
looked at him, really looked, and saw that the skinny
schoolkid had gone forever. There was a quiet
confidence about him that had almost ousted the
gawkiness without her noticing. She could postpone it
no longer. Trying to ignore Matt's approach to adult-

hood was, she saw, as useless as trying to deny his ambition. He would grow up and he would go his own way, as sons did, and she would have to let him, as mothers did. Even stepmothers. Still, acceptance didn't stop her hurting and, contrarily, she wanted to hurt him back.

'Hello,' she said brightly. 'Now *don't* tell me where you've been—you've been studying in the college library, right? Or maybe you've been at your best friend's place writing an assignment. How *hard* you work at your studies, Matt. Or should I call you "Chris"?'

He stiffened, and it was a blow to Darcie that he didn't bluster and make excuses like a schoolboy, but that he squared his shoulders and said quietly, with relief, 'You know. How did you find out?'

'I suppose you've managed to tear out anything about "Chris Reynolds" in the newspaper up until now, but you missed last Friday's. Dull-witted Darcie put two and two together at last. When were you planning to tell me about your secret life, Matt? Or were you going to leave that job to your new confidant, Mr Stafford?' She almost spat out this last, hurt beyond belief that he'd unburdened himself to the man.

'I'm sorry, Darcie. I didn't want to lie to you, but any time I even mentioned racing you started having those dreams again and crying out in your sleep, and I tried to forget all about it, honestly, because I didn't want to do that to you. I really tried. But I couldn't. I met someone at college with a racing car and I gofered for him and got some practice runs——' He spread his hands out in an eloquent gesture that reminded her so much of Gavin. Matt was going to be so much like him, and it was both pleasure and pain. 'And then I was offered a drive and I thought, just one, to see what it's like, and then I did it once more, and so on, and—I can't explain, but I *have* to do it, even if it hurts you, and I know that makes me a real jerk, but I——' He shrugged his shoulders helplessly. 'I'm sorry.'

Darcie went to him, full of remorse for her carping. Poor Matt, he couldn't explain because he still didn't realise the power of the fever in his blood. That he had it so badly rocked her, terrified her, but she knew what it was like and that there was no cure. Well, maybe only one. 'And I'm sorry too, Matt. If I'd faced up to facts sooner, you wouldn't have had to sneak around feeling guilty.' She put her arms around him. 'Forgive me. It's just that I'm so afraid for you.'

'And I for you, Darcie,' he said, hugging her tight. He sounded forty years old instead of seventeen. And Darcie wondered just which of them had been the guardian.

When Stafford had said he would 'wait and see' he hadn't had anything passive in mind, Darcie realised two weeks on. In spite of his heavy workload and the infighting at Ensigns, he took every opportunity to 'assess' Matt. Suddenly he loomed large in their lives, literally and metaphorically. Every time Darcie looked around, Patrick Stafford was there, filling her vision. She saw him almost every day in her rear-view mirror. Matt talked about him until her teeth were on edge. Stafford took the boy to his club, where they played billiards. Rick was brilliant at billiards. They played golf. Rick was great at golf. They worked on Matt's bike together. Rick used to ride a Harley-Davidson. The only thing Rick hadn't done, it seemed, was race cars. Rick held a pilot's licence, he had rowed competitively here and in the States, he played chess, tennis and the guitar, as she discovered one night when a metallic shriek had her rushing to the garage ready to give first aid. There she found Patrick with Matt's electric guitar slung around him on its gaudy purple and yellow strap while Matt fiddled with the amplifier's levels. 'Rick used to play guitar in a band,' Matt told her.

'I don't know how he found the time,' she said tartly. 'A rock band, I suppose?' Darcie imagined a scruffy group of boys with long hair and four chords between them.

'Jazz.' Patrick grinned at her and nonchalantly fingered a fast scale, followed by a few bars of 'That Old Black Magic'.

'Show off,' she said. He was good. Never had such a melodic sound come from Matt's guitar, but it didn't please her overmuch. Admiration shone from Matt's eyes and she turned away, irritated.

'What do you think?' Patrick called after her.

'Keep the guitar-strap,' she said. 'It looks a lot better around your neck than some of your ties!'

He did a chord-slide down the strings and the sound following her was a lot like electronic laughter. The ensuing sounds of their musical mateship reached her inside the house, and she half hoped that the neighbours would complain about the noise. It was churlish behaviour, she knew, and she was ashamed of herself. Stafford had put himself out for Matt, and Darcie, watching closely for any undue pressure, had to admit that he exerted no influence one way or another in the matter of racing. On the contrary, Patrick made it clear that he did not consider speed and recklessness any measure of a man, which was just as well, for Matt clearly wanted to impress him. She couldn't fault him. When Matt began talking about throwing in his business degree studies to take a job connected with the car industry, Patrick told him to forget it. It was the only point upon which they had come to argument. 'You might turn out to be a lousy driver,' Patrick said baldly, 'in which case you need a career back-up, and I don't mean selling used cars. If you *are* good enough, and lucky enough, to make it one day in professional racing, you'll make a lot of money, and a business degree will help you keep control of it. You don't want to be ripped off like your father.' Such brutal honesty sent Matt into a sulk. Matt, Darcie thought, was as much a stranger to brutal honesty as she was, but he adjusted, much faster than was necessary in Darcie's opinion.

The preliminary draft of Matt's contract with Ensigns was drawn up, and Darcie's solicitor went over it with a fine-tooth comb, suggested some minor alterations, and pointed out that there was a clause requiring her as well as Matt to use Ensigns products, and another restricting Darcie's use of her own professional image in any way construed as detrimental to Ensigns. 'You're happy about that?' he enquired, and Darcie said that, as she *had* no professional image any more, the clause was unnecessary, but she had no objection to it if Ensigns insisted on it. 'On the whole,' the solicitor said, 'it is favourable right down to the fine print. Matt's a lucky young man.'

The lucky young man went out and got drunk the next night. She was pacing the floor, on the verge of calling the police, when he turned up at two in the morning. Darcie was tight as a bowstring from anxiety. She was furious with him for drinking at all at his age, let alone into this state, but she could have put that aside, might even have found Matt's beaming, befuddled boasting funny, but for one thing. It was Patrick Stafford who brought him home.

'Matt called me,' he told her when she flung open the door to find him supporting her sozzled stepson with one arm, while with the other he used Matt's front door key. 'He knew he shouldn't drive, and couldn't trust his friends to drive safely, either, and had no money left for a cab.'

'I'm gonna be the best,' Matt called out to the slumbering neighbourhood, 'I'm gonna be famous. I'm gonna be a star.'

The Sorensons' dog howled.

'You're gonna have one hell of a headache,' Stafford said drily.

'Don't be angry with me, Darcie,' Matt beamed, his arm draped around Stafford's shoulder as the older man supported him inside. 'Had a few too many. Celebrating with some mates. Didn't drive, though. Knew I shouldn't drive.' He said it with simple pride, inviting her congratulations on his good sense. He blew her a kiss. 'Love you, Darcie. Wish I'd called you Mum, now. Didn't want to when I was a kid. Thought it sounded soppy. Can I call you Mum now?'

Stafford smiled. Darcie closed the door and ignored him. Icily, she looked at Matt. He'd needed help and he had called Patrick Stafford. Not her. Not the one who'd practically brought him up and filled the gap of ten motherless years, the one who'd made sure he ate right and slept eight hours every night and kept his shoulders back and didn't read in a bad light. Not the one who'd told him about sex and love and the dangers of drugs, the one who'd paced the floor for him. He hadn't called *her*. He'd called Stafford. She hated them both at that moment. The boy who'd betrayed her and the man who had somehow usurped her.

'It's a bit late to start calling me Mum,' she snapped. 'I don't suppose it bothers you that I've been waiting up, worried out of my mind?'

'Aw—Darcie . . .'

She followed them down the hall. 'How *dare* you stay out until all hours and come back in this condition? It's unforgivable, Matt, and I won't stand for it. I let you take my car, and then you leave it parked somewhere overnight because you're too drunk to drive it home again!'

Stafford lowered Matt on to his bed. The boy looked at Darcie like a doleful, hopeful clown. 'Sorry, Darcie.'

'This kind of behaviour makes me wonder about your intelligence. It certainly makes me think twice about trusting you. And, as from tonight, you're grounded. If you think I'm going to put up with——'

Stafford interrupted, gave Matt's shoulder a companionable shake. 'Goodnight, kid. Darcie is a bit upset. She was worried about you, that's all. Go to sleep.' He pulled the boy's shoes off and yanked the covers over him. 'OK, son?'

Son. *Son?* Darcie felt like the assistant for a bad knife-thrower. Sprawled on a revolving wheel in tights and spangles while he tossed daggers, every one missing the wheel, piercing her. 'A *bit* upset!' she burst out. 'Worried? I was out of my *mind*! And I had good reason to be, didn't I, when——?'

Stafford came over and clamped a massive hand over her mouth. 'Goodnight, Matt,' he said.

'G'night, Rick. G'night, Darcie—Mum,' Matt mumbled, and her heart contracted, but the only sounds she could make were furious muffled hoots into Stafford's oversized palm. She lashed out, but he hoisted her casually under one arm as if she were a slightly larger than average file and conveyed her to the kitchen.

'Why don't you give the kid a break?' he growled, putting her down.

Darcie was almost dancing with rage. 'How *dare* you gag me in my own home? How *dare* you interfere when——'

'Aw, quit nagging, will you? I didn't get up in the middle of the morning to do Matt a favour just to have you take your jealousy out on me.'

'Jealousy?' she squeaked. 'Don't make me laugh!'

'You're jealous as hell of me, Darcie,' he said tiredly, massaging the back of his neck. 'I know it, and so do you. Your little boy has grown up, he's about to make the last break from the apron-strings and has found a male influence he can relate to, and it's tying you up in knots. OK, I can sympathise. It takes time to adjust to a change like that, but for heaven's sake try not to nag the shine off Matt's glory. He's a young man and his ego is puffed way out of proportion, but it will soon get back to normal. It's natural for him to push a bit, test his wings——'

'He is *drunk*!' she hissed. 'Paralytic. He could have fallen in front of a car. He could have walked through a plate-glass window. He is seventeen and not of legal age and he is *drunk*!'

'Sure it's wrong. He's a young, irresponsible fool, and tomorrow he'll suffer for it. You've been worried and that's rough, but now he's safely home again. It's not a disaster.' His gaze roamed over her cotton pyjamas, her house-coat, her slippers. 'Your nightwear, I'm not so sure about. Where the devil did you dredge up those pyjamas? Real passion-killers.' He caught the edge of her house-coat and lifted it aside for a better look. 'The androgynous look, is it?'

She slapped his hand away. 'Get out! I don't want you here. I don't like you. I don't wish to be manhandled and lectured in my own home at two in the morning.'

She turned her back to show him the door, but he swung her around, looking and sounding as friendly as a grizzly bear.

'Lady, there are times when I can't find much to like in you, either. It may surprise you, but I've got better things to do at two in the morning than listen to the fish-wife carping of a frustrated mother-figure with the sex appeal of a wet sock!'

'Then go and do them!' she snapped, stung by his criticism. He made her sound middle-aged and sour and ungrateful. Guiltily, she knew she was being ungrateful, but words of thanks just choked in her throat.

'*You* should have better things to do——' he said, giving her a shake '—than arguing in the kitchen with a man about an eighteen-year-old kid! At two in the morning——' he said, enunciating every word with flinty deliberation '—a woman with your mouth and your legs should have other business with an unattached male, and I don't mean in the bloody kitchen, either!'

He gave her another small shake and glared at her, his face thrust close to hers. Static crackled in the air. Darcie couldn't drag her eyes from him. Tentatively, she pulled against his grip, but he transferred his hands to her waist. They were so large that they went nearly all the way around, and she drew in a sharp breath at the sudden enfolding intimacy, the flaring heat of his touch through her cotton pyjamas. He yanked her against him, and this time her gasp was audible. It seemed to please him, brought a glittering, purposeful look to his eyes. 'Maybe "wet sock" was a bit too strong,' he murmured.

CHAPTER FIVE

'I THINK . . .' she croaked.

He regarded her for a moment through half-closed eyes. 'What is it you think, Darcie?' he said softly, his breath warm on her mouth. She found she couldn't think at all. Only feel. The rise and fall of his chest, the drumbeat of his heart, the astonishing muscular mass of him impressed on her, the heat of his hands. At the last moment she turned her head, but he bent and kissed her neck instead of her mouth, and twined a hand in her hair to tilt her face towards him. That other time it had been she who took the initiative, and hazily she recalled his reluctant response—a brief, almost tentative exploration. The memory exploded. He kissed her with sensuous zest, caressing, licking at her lips, inviting a response that he couldn't know was locked away inside her. Yet her body swayed, her skin came alive to the glide of his hands, the rough texture of his clothes, and the faint rasp of his emerging beard. He sensed the change in her and played on it, rocked her hips against him with gentle earthiness, nuzzled aside her pyjama collar to rub his lips provocatively along her shoulder and slowly down into the hollow between her breasts. Slower still, watching her through half-closed eyes, he straightened and let her go. Trembling, Darcie leaned against the table for support. He regarded her for a moment, then dug into his trouser pocket.

'I left my car in the city and drove yours home so that you wouldn't be inconvenienced,' he said prosaically, tossing her car keys on to the table. 'Mind if I phone for a cab?'

Without waiting for her permission, he did so, and she was still stuck there at the table when she heard him replace the receiver, still rooted to the spot when he came back. His eyes narrowed and he seemed almost amused that she hadn't moved. Leaning in the doorway, he crossed his arms, hitched one ankle in front of the other, and studied her silently. For long moments she stared back at him across the kitchen, before the colour rushed to her face and she shot upright, following his gaze to her chest. A pyjama button had come undone, and the jacket plunged revealingly to her waist. Darcie fumblingly fixed it, then wrapped her dressing-gown close around her, grasped the sash in both hands, and tightened it with a savage little jerk.

Stafford observed all these signals and grinned. 'I'll wait outside.'

He let himself out, and only minutes later she heard the cab pull up. When it had gone again she sank into an armchair. If it had been his intention to shock her, then he had achieved his purpose. He had touched her, kissed her with the same frankness that characterised his speech, and she knew that shouldn't shock her, but it did. Physical frankness was something else again. He had wanted her. A man couldn't hide the fact, and he hadn't even tried to do so. Some small, vain part of her preened that she had aroused his desire. Even, she thought with malicious satisfaction, the passion-killer pyjamas hadn't dampened his interest. The gratification didn't last.

Rather, she was jolted by the proof that he found her sexually desirable. It set her mind wandering along paths she felt ill-equipped to travel, it made her think of things she hadn't considered in three years of widowhood. Being wanted as a woman had been central to her life for so long, being needed by a man a fantastic, frustrating, satisfying, problematic but essential part of her being. Without it, she realised now, part of her had dried up, like her French perfume, left sitting unused on the dressing-table. Darcie gazed into space. Life without that part of her was simple, and she didn't know if she was ready to have it stirred again.

Too late, she acknowledged hours later as she tried in vain to sleep. Ready or not, it had been stirred, and by Patrick Stafford, and Darcie's mind and body were in a state of mixed celebration and retreat. Eventually she slept and didn't dream at all. Or, if she did, she didn't remember.

It the morning, while Matt nursed his hangover and made vows never to have one again, Darcie took an excited phone call from her brother.

'It's a boy!' he yelled down the line from Mackay. 'I was there when he was born, and I've never seen anything like it in my life. Darcie, it was a miracle . . . We're calling him Stephen James and we're going to have another three kids a.s.a.p. and we want you to be godmother . . .'

'What—to them all?' she laughed.

Afterwards she stood before her notice-board, smiling at the photograph of Martin and pregnant Sara. And now they were three, she thought. 'Martin says they're going to have four children,' she told

Matt, who did his best to rouse some enthusiasm. 'He makes it sound quite urgent, as if they might run out of time. But Sara's only twenty-two . . .' Darcie looked through the kitchen window to a trellis full of yellow roses. I am twenty-seven, she thought, with a Rip van Winkle feeling of having just woken up and discovered the fact. Twenty-seven.

Later, of course, she apologised to Patrick for giving him such a cold reception when he'd interrupted his sleep to bring Matt home. She chose to pretend the kiss in the kitchen had never happened, and he apparently chose to allow her to pretend, for though he looked at her mockingly now and then, he said nothing about it. The kitchen had a new ambience. Now, she thought resentfully, even the preparation of a steak and kidney pie made her think of Patrick.

He went away for a week on a business trip shortly afterwards to visit some country tanneries with the object of buying one or more. 'To maintain supply and quality of leathers for our medium range—not our prestige line, of course, we import our top leathers from Scotland.' Mark gave a dyspeptic smile. 'All Patrick's idea. He thinks it's a clever financial move.'

'And is it?'

He engaged in a small mental struggle, and honesty won over pride. 'I nearly choke on the words but, yes, it is. We should have made the move long ago.'

'It takes a big uncle to admit it,' Darcie said, smiling.

'He has an instinct for what needs to be done. I've been in the business thirty-five years and he pays me the courtesy of asking my advice, but I suspect he doesn't need it.'

Darcie nodded sympathetically. Patrick had a way of

making others feel redundant. Hadn't she experienced it herself, watching his handling of Matt?

'If only there was something he *wasn't* good at!' Mark said, and instantly looked ashamed at the childish wish.

'Take heart,' she grinned, 'he's a terrible dresser.'

His appearance, when she picked him up in the Rolls on his return from the country, reinforced the description. He wore faded jeans and a T-shirt, and a battered leather flying jacket. Patrick had not sedately travelled business-class air, as all other Ensigns executives did. He had chartered a small aircraft and flown himself.

When she saw him coming towards the Rolls; toting an overnight bag, Darcie felt an amazing sense of gladness. She had missed him, she realised now—missed seeing those lopsided eyes in her rear-view mirror, missed finding him at her front door, missed his dry humour and his irritating frankness and the sound of his growling voice. He saw her and smiled broadly, and Darcie felt she was caught in a torch beam—not of light, but of warmth.

He kept right on coming, hooked an arm around her waist and swung her off the ground in a half-circle, tossing his bag into the Rolls's open boot in one fluid move as he set her down again. Darcie tottered a bit, breathless at this exuberant display of strength, and for a few moments was held close in his arms, experiencing that beam of warmth from close quarters. It was too close, scorching, and she dragged her eyes from his, down to his mouth and swiftly away as his smile faded and he released her.

'Very acrobatic,' she said when he released her,

primly adjusting her cap to hide her confusion.

He waved her away as she made to open the door for him, and moved around instead to the other side of the car. 'Flying brings out the boy in me,' he said, presumably to explain his exuberance. Darcie got the impression that he had rather surprised himself with that boisterous greeting.

'Sounds dangerous,' she said.

He waited a moment, his hand on the front door handle, staring at her across the gleaming top of the Rolls. Then his mouth quirked in a half-smile.

'Only when I come down again,' he said, and he got into the back seat.

Funny, that. Darcie had the feeling that he'd been planning to sit in the front with her and changed his mind. On the whole, she thought, discreetly closing the glass partition between them, she was glad.

The weeks passed. There were photographs of wizened, hairless Stephen James on the notice-board now, along with glowing reports of his weight gains and precociousness.

Matt was nearly eighteen, and any faint hope that he might lose interest in racing, or prove temperamentally unsuited, had long since faded. Apart from his one night of drinking, he had shown maturity and common sense and the will to work. He gofered for several drivers and mechanics, and earned and begged his way behind the wheel of their cars. Darcie steeled herself and went to watch his next drive. He came fourth that day in a car that suffered clutch trouble from start to finish. Another time she watched him do some practice laps.

Alone she stood on the grass, swamped by a wave of nostalgia. On this day of sunshine, with the drone of a single car and the low revs of others, with silence from the empty spaces behind the barricades, she was overcome with a longing to return. But it was mingled with fear and guilt as she pictured the same scene packed with people, and not just one car but many hurtling around the track. Perspiration broke out on her brow and she dabbed at it with a tissue, forcing herself to stay there to watch Matt as he lapped again in the metallic blue Sierra.

There was so much of her life bonded to places like this—her achievements, her youth. Patrick had stirred an atrophied part of her, and this place stirred another. Two big parts of her life, missing. She wondered which of the two would take more courage to reinstate.

'Would you like to drive again, Darcie?' a voice said behind her. A familiar voice that sent another surge of adrenalin into her system. He was in jeans and a cotton shirt under stress, and had a twill bomber-jacket slung over one shoulder. The breeze ruffled his hair and he smiled at her, and her heart bounced about like a tennis ball. Had she thought he had no looks? Astonishing. The man was dynamite, with that craggy jawline and those big white teeth and silvery-grey eyes. Darcie steadied herself. He was Patrick and, as usual, asking questions she'd rather not answer.

'I do drive—every day,' she said lightly.

'Really drive, I mean. Not the milk-run stuff you do for me.' He squinted at Matt's car, matchbox-small and shimmering in the distance. 'Do you think about it? How good it was—how good you were?'

'No to all questions,' she said. 'I don't think about it at all.'

'Sounds unnatural.'

'I *used* to think about it,' she admitted, deeming it wise to temper her reply, 'when I first retired. But it was a long time ago.'

'Why did you retire?'

Darcie's temper stirred. 'I told you—I retired when I got married.'

'Ah, yes,' he murmured, and quoted, ' "There isn't room in a marriage for two professional drivers." '

The faint trace of scepticism didn't escape her. He was too clever. 'It's true. Anyway, it's none of your business what I think or what I've done in the past.'

'I just can't resist asking,' he told her gravely. 'It goes back to my childhood. I was always in trouble because I had to look behind doors that said "No Entry". Always had to trespass where there was a "No Trespassers" sign.'

'What a rotten kid you must have been.'

'A brat. I was Hyde and Michael was Jekyll.'

'Michael?'

'My brother,' he said. 'My twin. He died when we were eight.'

'Oh. How awful for you,' she said inadequately, and fell silent for a moment. 'Jekyll and Hyde? Could twins be that different?'

'We were fraternal twins, like Mark and my mother, not identical. Not even similar. Michael was a true Stafford. Good-looking, charming, an accomplished pianist—the kind of kid parents bring out to show off to guests.' He gave a short laugh. 'In the one package they got Michael and me. A little joke of the Creator's.' He slanted a look down at her. 'I was rarely requested to make an appearance when we had guests.'

Michael, she decided, must have been a near genius to

cast Patrick in the shade. 'That's terrible,' she frowned. 'That's not fair.'

He shrugged. 'I was clumsy, rebellious and usually dirty. A real misfit in the Stafford clan. It was another joke of the Creator's that the wrong twin died.'

'Don't!' Darcie exclaimed. 'You shouldn't say that.'

'Why not? Everyone else did,' he said with irony.

'Everyone? You don't mean your parents said that?'

He looked amused at her shocked expression, and didn't answer.

'Sometimes children misinterpret things that adults say,' she suggested, wanting to offer him a way out of such a terrible belief.

He gave a wry smile. 'I tried to tell myself that, but I never could believe in fairy-tales, even as a child.'

Unlike her, he meant. Darcie flushed. 'It's hard for a child who can't believe in fairy-tales.'

There was an infinitesimal tightening along his jaw. 'Oh, yes, it's murder.' He reached out suddenly and rubbed at her frown-line with the pad of his thumb. 'Your distress on my behalf is very moving, but unnecessary. I'm a big boy now. It's ancient history.'

His fingers brushed along her temple, swiftly, delicately down her cheek, leaving a tingling sensation in their wake.

' "In our past lies our present"—I'm quoting someone misquoting someone else,' she said.

'*Touché,* sweetheart.' Patrick laughed. Even so, she got a vague impression of defences going up. 'Doing anything Tuesday night?'

Darcie was instantly off balance. 'Tuesday? Oh—er —I . . .'

'Yes, I know you have to wash your hair, and other

clichés,' he said drily, 'but I'm not asking you to dinner again, just want to know if you can work late.'

Feeling rather foolish, she stiffly asked about the job. He and Mark had to attend a cocktail party at Palm Beach, he said, and such was the importance of Barry Prenzler, the client, that they had to make a showing with the Rolls. It would mean she would have to kill a couple of hours waiting for them, he said. Was that a problem? No problem, she said.

The Prenzler place was perched on a rocky ledge high above the street, with the sea way down below and beyond it. Darcie guided the Rolls up the steep drive and into a covered forecourt to unload her passengers. As Mark stepped out he pulled a face and rubbed gently at his midriff. 'Late lunch. Curried prawns,' he confided, and Darcie, accustomed to the burps and hiccups of chronic executive indigestion, offered him some antacid tablets from the glove compartment. He took two and squeezed her arm in thanks.

'We won't be long, my dear. Patrick and I have discovered an important area of agreement. We both hate cocktail parties.'

Nevertheless, it was nearly two hours before they reappeared, and they seemed to have opened up another area for agreement, because they were talking amiably over some minor point raised by their host. Mark opened the partition as they drove away and requested the antacid.

'The cocktail party,' he sighed. 'What sort of an invention *was* that?'

'Nowhere to sit, pretend food, pretend conversation, and a photographer to record pretend friendships,' Patrick said. 'Must have been a political invention.'

Mark laughed and leaned forward to pass the box of antacid tablets back to Darcie. In the intermittent light from the street lamps his face looked pale and clammy.

'Mark, do you feel all right?' she asked.

'I should never have eaten the pretend canapés,' he grimaced.

Prosaically, Patrick asked if he wanted to stop the car.

'No, no—don't fuss!' But he gave a grunt of pain and clutched at his chest even as he leaned back in the seat.

'Mark? What is it?'

'Often get a few twinges—it's nothing . . .' But a minute later perspiration was beading his brow, and he doubled over. Alarmed, Darcie pulled into the kerb, but Patrick, bending over his uncle, said sharply to her, 'Keep going. He's passed out. Where's the nearest hospital?'

He was dialling on the car phone before she'd finished telling him. 'Step on it, Darcie!' With the phone clenched between his neck and shoulder he loosened Mark's clothing, shrugged out of his own jacket and spread it over him. Into the phone he snapped emergency details—what hospital they were heading for, the patient's symptoms. 'Indigestion pain,' she heard him say. 'No, there is no family history of heart trouble.'

But that didn't mean it wasn't his heart. Darcie licked her lips and checked Mark in the rear-view mirror. His face was contorted, deathly pale. The emergency operator must have asked Patrick if he wanted to transfer the patient to an ambulance. 'No, we could lose too much time.' He looked up to meet Darcie's eyes in the mirror. 'We have a professional driver who can get him to hospital quicker than an ambulance, anyway.'

'I'm not——' she said shakily.

'You bloody well are! So stop quivering and do the only thing you can do to help him. Drive!' Patrick slammed the partition shut and Darcie was suddenly alone.

'Bastard!' she said between the clenched edges of her teeth, her eyes wide and staring. She took a deep breath, then another, and the panic paled. Her brain made the shift until she didn't think about Mark at all, only the distance she had to travel and the shortest possible time in which she could safely cover it. Coldly she reviewed her mental map of the area and plotted short cuts away from major traffic. Her foot went down on the accelerator, and the Rolls answered with an eager new note in its voice. Every car had its own voice. In the old days they'd told her things. A ragged note here, a deeper resonance here, and she would go over an engine again with the mechanics who had mocked her 'woman's intuition', but they'd grown to respect it. In the old days. With her hand on the horn she accelerated into a corner and swerved so close around a parked truck that it rocked. Into a one-way street and out again, horn blasting all the way. Some of these streets she'd never used, but once Darcie had seen a map she remembered what was on it. Another gift. One that had remained with her. The Rolls flew.

Someone had once calculated that a driver performed some fifty or sixty manoeuvres in an average lap, at speeds unknown to the ordinary driver. Each manoeuvre needed four or five mental operations, and as many physical ones. To anyone else it would be a constant emergency. To professional drivers it became a way of life, a high on which they thrived. She hadn't forgotten.

Darcie sped through a radar trap, ignoring the wild signals of the police, and when a road patrol motorcycle roared up, siren wailing in pursuit, she ignored that, too. the hospital was in sight, and she concentrated on making it to the finish.

In the ambulance bay Mark was transferred on to a stretcher and wheeled inside, surrounded by running casualty staff. Patrick went with them, and Darcie, still cool, drove the Rolls away and parked it. The motorcycle cop stared at her. When he had seen they had an emergency on their hands, he had tried to overtake to give them an escort. But he had had to escort them, siren screaming, from behind. 'Boy, I'll never joke about women drivers again! Can I have your name for the record?'

'Darcie Miller,' she said, and felt her icy calm begin to break up. 'I mean Brooke. Darcie Brooke.'

By the time she found Patrick, she was shaking. She saw him silhouetted at the end of a long corridor, and she started to go down it, dreading the news, going faster and faster to reach him. He looked up and came to her, powering along the glossy, polished surface to catch her by the waist. It was like being anchored suddenly to a rock pillar.

'Not a heart attack. Ulcer,' he said economically, 'duodenal, perforated. He's gone into theatre. There's nothing we can do but wait.'

They went and drank coffee from a machine. Patrick phoned his mother with the news. In a small room with armchairs and magazines and ashtrays they passed the time by talking about Mark, as if by mentioning his name often it kept him earthbound, alive. Neither of them acknowledged that people sometimes died from ruptured ulcers. Darcie phoned Matt, declining his offer to join her. 'Come tomorrow when you can speak to Uncle Mark,' she said, firmly creating an image of Mark, sitting up in bed, talking to visitors. They waited until he was out of theatre and out of danger. Then Patrick made more phone calls to pass on the good news, and they went home.

Patrick drove this time, taking the keys from her without comment and showing her into the front passenger seat.

'I'll take the Rolls back to the office and pick up my own car. You can take a cab to work in the morning.'

She nodded, remembering that she had parked her own car in Ensigns' basement an age ago, that morning. In silence, Patrick walked up the front path with her. She was shaking again, worse than before. 'It's reaction,' he said softly, taking her by the shoulders. 'Have you got some brandy?'

Darcie looked up at him numbly. 'We should have called an ambulance. I could have hurt someone, driving like that . . .'

He frowned. 'Hurt someone?'

'Driving like that—I could have blanked out again—lost it—I might have killed someone . . .'

Patrick's eyes narrowed on her. 'But you didn't lose it. And you didn't hurt anyone. You might even have saved Mark's life.'

She shook her head wildly. 'You should have sent for an ambulance. Why didn't you? Why did you rely on me?'

'Because I believe in Darcie Miller,' he said, and he pulled her close and cradled her head against his chest. 'Tell me about your last race,' he said softly.

'It's all in the files.'

'I wonder,' he murmured. She shook her head and pushed him away. Tried to, anyway. Immovable, that was him. Built like a tank. 'You'll tell me eventually.'

'No,' she said into his shirt. It was an awful shirt, but it was much better from this viewpoint. It smelled so nice, for one thing. *He* smelled so nice. He always did, she realised.

'You'll tell me everything eventually,' he said, with a smile in his voice.

'Are you trying to hypnotise me?' she asked. ' "You will tell me everything."?' She tried to work up some steam about it, but couldn't somehow. Shock and reaction had made her weak, dazed, bereft even of the energy to release herself from this sustained bear-hug. He chuckled, and the sound and vibration of it was like a minor earthquake beneath her ear. Such a solid man, she thought. She'd been wrong ever to imagine that he might be running to seed. Her hands moved a little to spread on his lower back, so that the channel of his spine was at the tips of her middle fingers. No flab, just tough muscle and bone. Lots of it. Her body warmed. Three years was such a long, long time. He was strong, intensely masculine, and Darcie felt a sudden piercing need to be loved again. He had stirred that subdued part of her, and now, in a rush, it exploded in desire. She moved against him, flexed her fingers and caught at the fabric of his shirt, before she checked herself. Darcie stiffened, horrified at the involuntary invitation she'd offered. But maybe he hadn't noticed. Patrick released her with a matter-of-fact, 'Go inside and have that brandy. Goodnight.'

'Goodnight,' she said, and watched him walk to the

Rolls. Thank heaven he hadn't noticed!

Matt was working on his bike in the garage. 'Uncle Mark?' he queried.

'He'll be OK,' she said, and stood there watching him as they discussed Mark's collapse. Eventually she said, 'Matt—has Patrick ever talked to you about the possibility of me driving again? Real driving, I mean—not the milk-run stuff I do now.' She bit her lip to hear herself using his own phrase.

Matt showed signs of annoyance with his hero. 'Has he said something to you about it? I told him to forget it. I told him not to say anything to you because it would upset you and start up the dreams again.' Frowning, he wiped his hands and tossed the rag on to the floor. 'Bloody hell—it's bad enough you've had to get used to me racing. I told him I didn't want you upset any further.'

Darcie nodded absently. 'I wish you wouldn't swear, Matt. Swearing stunts your vocabulary. Why would Patrick want me to drive again?'

He shrugged. 'I don't know maybe he thinks it's a waste of talent if you don't—maybe he thinks it would make for better promotion for Ensigns. I mean, if both you and I were racing, it would get double the interest from the media—Gavin Brooke's son starting out and Gavin Brooke's ex-champion widow,' he said pragmatically. 'You can't blame sponsors for making sure they get coverage. They provide the money, after all——' Matt stopped abruptly. 'Of course, Rick never said anything like that, Darcie. I'm just guessing.'

'You guess is as good as mine,' she said wryly.

The hospital's morning bulletin on Mark was positive. Mr Rawlinson was resting comfortably and could see visitors. She took a cab to the office and was informed that Mr Stafford wanted her to pick him up in the Rolls at his home this morning. The other drivers raised their brows and made a few crude jokes about her being so much in demand with the bigwigs, and Darcie had half a mind to ask for a job-swap and send Bill in her stead. Curiosity stopped her. She wanted to see where Patrick lived.

It was unprepossessing, to say the least, she decided, as she parked outside the scaffolding-sheathed building. Rough brick, two-storeys high, with a battered concrete forecourt and no garden. She dodged beneath the ladders and rather tentatively selected one of the many doors to knock on. While she waited an express train went by unseen, a few streets away. The door flung open as if it were in the grip of some gargantuan monster, which it was. Patrick stood there, his face half-lathered in shaving foam, his chest bare, a towel swathed about his hips.

'Morning, Darcie. Come in.'

She blinked, hesitated. His bare, brawny chest, spattered with dark brown hair, was not what she expected to see at eight forty-five in the morning. Or any time. She dragged her eyes upwards and found him watching her with great interest and amusement. 'Come in,' he said, and, taking her arm, walked her into an interior in which the essential comforts were grouped in a cleared island of floor, surrounded by renovation clutter and packing-cases full of books and pictures.

'Sit down. I won't be long.'

He strode off, looking broader than ever, his back and shoulder muscles rippling as he moved. His legs were predictably stalwart and hairy, and the towel, carelessly draped over his behind, had an odd sort of sculptural effect. No elegance, none at all, but he could have been a stand-in for Charlton Heston in *Ben Hur*. Rather irritated with herself, Darcie wandered around, picking up one or two books from the open packing-cases. A framed photograph caught her eye and she twisted around idly to look at it. Curiosity got the better of her, and she pulled the picture out from between the books. There were actually two photographs in the frame, fairly obviously taken on the same day. In the first, Patrick was rowing in a kayak, giving his all in a race. In the second, the race was over, and Patrick, his skin gleaming with perspiration, was pictured with a towel around his neck and his arm around a pretty brunette.

Patrick reappeared just then to fling open a cupboard and take out a hand-towel, with which he dabbed at his shaved face. He walked over to see what she held.

'Lake Michigan,' he informed her. 'I won a trophy that day.'

Darcie looked at the girl's adoring face and bit back a fairly obvious retort. Politely, she asked about his kayak racing, and, rather gravely, he answered. At last she had to ask.

'Who's the girl?'

'She took the pictures—the second was a delayed shot. She's a photographer. We lived together for a time.'

'A nice, warm, stable woman with plenty of passion?' she mocked, speaking before she thought.

'Uh-huh.' He raised his brows and waited for further questions. If he thought she was going to ask his ex-girlfriend's name, he could think again. Damping down her curiosity, she changed tack.

'I suppose kayak racing is one reason you're so——'

she looked at his Ben Hur arms and his frankly amused eyes'—so over-developed around the shoulders. I imagine you'd put on condition very quickly in a sport like that.'

'Very quickly,' he said with that annoying gravity. 'A whole shirt size in about six months.'

But Darcie was looking again at the photograph, and wondering about Patrick living with this adoring brunette. From the way he spoke, it was all over without breakages. He walked away again and called back over his shoulder, 'Her name is Theresa.'

Scowling, she dropped the framed pictures back where she found them. A thunderous banging from above brought her head up.

'The renovators are up there, working their way down,' Patrick yelled, presumably from the bathroom. 'They've put in the mezzanine floor, and I'm making do down here until they've finished the bedroom partitioning. Then I can move upstairs while they do this floor.'

Darcie looked around, seeing beyond the litter and abuse of years to the solid worth of the interior. The outside might be lacking in dash, but the building had an interesting beamed roof and the sort of tough integrity of one constructed for sound, practical reasons. Handled sympathetically, it could be really something. But it would need the right materials, the right colours.

'Who chose everything?' she asked, looking at a stack of unopened paint-tins.

'What was that?' he called, as a train shot past, the clackety-clack of carriages following the initial blast.

Darcie walked towards the bathroom, the better to hear him over the racket of the passing train. 'I said, who chose your colour scheme—oh! Sorry.' She came to an abrupt halt in the doorway of a makeshift bedroom. While she'd been gazing up at his roof, he'd left the bathroom, and was pulling on trousers over rather graphic black underpants.

'Don't bolt,' he said calmly, zipping his trousers. 'You've seen a man dress before. I chose everything myself. Paint, papers, carpets. I designed the alterations, too.'

Darcie hovered in the doorway, unwilling to appear girlishly coy by rushing away when the man was so offhand. 'Oh, really?' she said, with a touch of dryness. If his taste in furnishing was anything like his taste in clothes, the old place would turn out a mess. He went on talking casually, as if he was accustomed to dressing in front of an audience. Darcie watched him pick two matching socks out from a drawer full of unattached ones. He was as bad as Matt, she thought.

'I bought this place five years ago, before I went to work in Chicago,' he told her, sitting on the bed to haul on the socks. 'A friend of mine rented the place while I was gone, which meant I could leave a lot of stuff here in storage. Lucky, too, as it happened, because my luggage——' he broke off, sending her an amused, calculating sort of glance as he bent to adjust the toe of one sock '—had to be put somewhere.' His shoes were generally of much better quality than his clothes, she thought, watching him tie his laces. Perhaps the size of his feet forced him to have shoes custom-made.

'Would you mind telling me why I'm here?'

'I want to call at the hospital, and thought you might like to come along and see Mark, too. After that you can drive me to a number of appointments. I don't expect we'll be back in the office until late afternoon.'

'Oh, terrific!' she muttered. 'They're going to love that.'

'Who?'

'The other drivers. My car in the basement overnight and me arriving by taxi to pick up the Rolls to come to *your* place—which I wish you hadn't broadcast, by the way—and then neither of us showing up again till afternoon.'

'You think there'll be talk?' he said mildly. 'So what? You've weathered it before.'

'Thanks very much. It's going to make me look—well, one rumour hasn't much substance. Two, and people start saying that there's no smoke without fire. I'm old-fashioned, and I dislike having my reputation dissected on the grapevine.'

'You're making too much of it. Just suppose you and I *were* having an affair——' He paused, holding her gaze. A million images flitted through her mind. 'Apart from the fact that I'm the boss and you're my driver, it's hardly scandalous, is it? We're both of age and unattached. If I have a woman in my life it doesn't raise any eyebrows, and the same must surely apply to you? There must have been a man or two in your life since you were widowed, even allowing for the passion-killer pyjamas.'

Darcie opened her mouth and shut it again.

'Well, one man, anyway,' he amended.

'None of your business.'

His eyes narrowed. 'No boyfriends at all?'

'No comment,' she said frostily.

He gave a long-drawn-out whistle, stuck his hands on his hips, and studied her anew. 'You're a passionate woman. Three years is a long time to be on your own.'

'On my own?' she hooted. 'Without a man, you mean. A typical male reaction! Why is it that men assume a widow is automatically passionate and pining for a man?'

'I'm not assuming,' he said mildly. 'You kissed me, remember?'

'I did not,' she snapped. 'You did it all by yourself—I certainly didn't respond.'

'Before that. In the park. The day you kidnapped me.'

Darcie flushed. 'Oh, that. I was—disorientated. I thought you were Gavin.'

Those lopsided, ambiguous eyes never let her go for a moment. Softly, he said, 'And who did you think I was last night?'

Her face was on fire now. She thought he hadn't noticed. The humiliation was agonising. 'I don't know what you mean.'

'Sure you do,' he stated with irritating assurance. 'Why so embarrassed? You fancied me. Nothing wrong with that.'

His cool arrogance rescued her from embarrassment. 'Fancied you? Why, you conceited—— I was married to a man in a million. Gavin had it all—looks, charisma, talent—he was a *sex-symbol*. Why do you think there's been no one else? Because no one else can live up to that——'

'Oh, no, that won't wash,' he said, smiling, but she could see he was annoyed, as she'd meant him to be. 'You're too intelligent to believe you can only ever fancy men in Gavin's mould.'

'I wish you'd stop saying *fancy*,' she snapped. 'It makes me sound like some little tart, going about *fancy-*

ing men.'

'*Wanted*, then. You wanted me last night,' he said softly, and it sounded a lot worse. He stretched out and, with his arm fully extended, traced his forefinger from her forehead, down the side of her face to her chin. His hand stayed there, but his eyes went on, evocatively continuing the caress down her body. 'And I wanted you.'

Combined exhilaration and fear licked along her nerve-ends. The air was suddenly criss-crossed with currents and messages, and Darcie was relieved when another mighty thud from the mezzanine broke up the atmosphere.

Patrick went to a wardrobe, selected a shirt without fuss, then pulled it on. Her eyes lingered on the dark felting that grew wall-to-wall on his chest. Vaguely, she wondered what it was like to touch. Leaving his shirt buttons unfastened, he reached for a Paisley tie. It slithered through his big hands like a psychedelic snake, and it was too much for Darcie.

'No, please, not that one,' she entreated, taking one end of it. 'There are people out there on the brink of manic depression. People contemplating ending it all. You don't want to be the one to push them over.'

'You told me it suited me perfectly.'

'I stand by that opinion.'

He laughed, and let her take the offending tie away and select another less awful. There was something pleasing about seeing him button his shirt and tuck it in, then flip his tie over as he knotted it. She felt a poignant longing for the small, masculine rituals that had been part of marriage. A man shaving, fixing his tie, shrugging on a jacket and flexing his shoulders into it in the distinctive way men had. Oh, Matt did some of that, it was true, but it wasn't the same. Now that her grief had passed it was the small, foolish things she missed. A pair of running-shoes in the bedroom. Pyjama bottoms under the pillow. Loose change and credit cards strewn on the dressing-table. She wrenched her gaze from a large pair of running-shoes on the carpet.

'I'll wait in the car,' she said.

CHAPTER SIX

MARK was pale and weak, but in good spirits. He thanked Darcie for beating all her previous lap times to get him to the hospital, he demanded the quarterly budget spreadsheets from Patrick, and rang for the nurse to bring him some fresh iced water. He told Darcie she looked better than she had for years, and just in time, too, now that she was in the news again. He winced at Patrick's tie, and said he could donate his awful clothes to charity soon surely, because hadn't his secretary said yesterday that his proper ones had turned up in Munich?

'Yes, Uncle Mark,' Patrick said, patting the older man's arm soothingly. To Darcie he said, 'Must be the anaesthetic in his system.'

But Mark was right about one thing. She was in the news again. Only minutes later a reporter and photographer materialised by the bedside, to get a picture of her with Patrick and Mark for the 'mercy dash' story. 'Great,' the reporter said, 'you're in your chauffeur's uniform. Just tip the cap back a little bit, hmm?'

The unexpectedness of it, and Patrick's restraining arm around her shoulder, prevented Darcie's escape. 'I don't wish to be part of this . . .' she said between her teeth.

'You *are* part of it.'

'You pig—if you don't let me go, I'll . . .'

But he didn't let her go. In the photograph in the evening paper, she looked stiff and strained. Ms Darcie Miller, the accompanying report went, was 'reluctant' to talk about her mercy dash to the hospital. The former race and rally driver, who retired on her marriage to Grand Prix champion Gavin Brooke, tragically killed in a race at Hockenheim, was 'modest' about her career, and 'non-committal' about a possible comeback to coincide with her stepson Matt Brooke's launch into amateur racing under Ensigns' sponsorship. Which, in newspaper jargon, meant that she hadn't said anything at all. But someone had. Someone had alerted them to the story; someone had told them about Matt. Someone who stood to gain from it. Sick at heart, Darcie recalled Patrick's arm tight around her, forcing her to pose for the photograph.

'Ensigns are reaping the publicity already,' she said in a high voice to Matt. She was angry, she was vulnerable, now that her precious anonymity had been stripped from her, but most of all she was disappointed. 'I should have known,' she said. 'Patrick was never going to be the selfless benefactor. He wants his pound of flesh in return for your sponsorship.'

Matt's mouth set grimly. He went to the phone and Darcie heard the murmur of his voice, angry at first, gradually lowering, until it ceased altogether. When he came back he was smiling.

'It's OK. I didn't think Rick would purposely put you in the firing-line like that. It was the motorcycle cop who told the newspaper. The reporter is a pal of his, apparently. He phoned someone at Ensigns and got the stuff about me.'

It was good enough for Matt. But not for Darcie. Matt

went to visit Mark in the hospital and she paced around the house, wishing she had not let him take the car. At length she stalked to her bedroom, snatched her Ensigns uniforms and jacket from the wardrobe, and thrust them into a paper bag. The chauffeur's cap followed, then she went to the garage and stuffed the lot into the bike's saddlebag. If he wasn't at home, she thought as she roared down the street on the Kawasaki, she would dump the parcel on his doorstep. He would get the message.

Not only was he at home, he was expecting her. Before she'd parked the bike he was leaning in the open doorway, big and burly in black jeans and a faded, green cotton sweater. He looked like a nightclub bouncer, but from behind him came the fluting sound of an aria from *Madame Butterfly* to throw doubt on the image.

He eyed her leather bike-jacket, her gloves and crash helmet. 'Well, well,' he drawled, 'it's the wild one.'

Darcie flipped up her visor and looked coldly at him, 'Matt thinks of you as a friend and needs your backing, and I have to live with that, but I don't have to work for you. I resign, Patrick.' She lobbed the parcel of uniforms at his feet.

Patrick regarded it with mild interest. 'Now that you've made your dramatic gesture, why don't we talk about it?'

'There's nothing to talk about. But don't imagine you'll get away with any of your shabby self-promotion tricks once Matt turns eighteen. Don't forget that I'm named as adviser on all matters concerning Matt's career, and if you think you'll use him you can—— Ouch! Let go!' For a big man he moved like greased lightning. He grabbed a handful of the leather jacket and wheeled

Darcie inside, retrieving and tossing the parcel unceremoniously on to the floor beside a clutter of paint-tins. The door slammed.

'I will repeat what I said to Matt,' he said harshly. 'I did not ring the newspaper with the tale of your "mercy dash". Why should I? I have highly paid professionals working on a sophisticated, structured campaign involving Matt. Why the hell would I want this petty little piece of exposure?'

'If you didn't, why would you use duress to make me pose for that photo?' she demanded. 'You know how I feel about publicity—you know that I hate all that and . . . you could have let me slip away.'

'You've made slipping away into an art form.'

'Well, you got what you wanted. A nice little human interest story to link Ensigns with Matt and milk a bit more mileage out of Gavin's crash!' Her voice choked a bit in sheer fury. 'I've managed to stay out of the limelight all this time, and now you've put me right in it. Don't try it again. I still have *some* influence with Matt, and that contract isn't signed yet!'

He fairly blazed. Darcie inched steadily backwards as he advanced on her. 'Two weeks and it will be, Darcie. But just don't push me too far. However good he is, Matt won't get a deal like the one we're offering him—it works both ways. We're giving a lot and we expect a lot in return——' contemptuously he overrode her interjection about pounds of flesh '—and that includes some trust. By now, I would have thought you would *know* I wouldn't do anything to—oh, for Pete's sake!' he roared in exasperation. 'Will you stop creeping backwards? And stop looking as if I'm about to thrash you!' He reached out to her, but she jerked away, unnerved by his black expression and his hunching shoulders. 'Look out! There's a tin of paint behind you—you'll trip——'

She tripped. The paint-tin tipped with a tinny sound, and the lid must have been loose, for it came off. Darcie, more intent on keeping her balance than on the pool of aubergine-coloured paint lapping at her feet, miscalculated and slipped. Down she went, her right foot leaving a long dark smear on the floorboards.

'Aaah!' she yelled. Her helmeted head hit the floor with a crack that exploded in her ears. Stunned, she gazed up unblinkingly as Patrick dropped to his knees beside her.

'Darcie.' He waved his hand before her eyes and she couldn't blink. He looked very worried, she thought vaguely. All that paint wasted. His hands shook as he lifted her head and removed the helmet. 'Dammit, Darcie—I tried to tell you . . .' His eyes were very dark, all pupil and just a thin rim of silvery-grey, and his face was sober with concern. Really, he was almost handsome at times. Gently, thoroughly, he checked her neck and skull and Darcie closed her eyes, soothed by the sure movements of his hands in her hair.

'Say something, Darcie,' he urged, bending close to her so that she felt his breath surge across her chin. She opened her eyes and gazed at him.

'You should never have picked the colours yourself,' she croaked, indicating the aubergine pool. 'It's horrible.'

He gave a huff of laughter that was part relief, but he didn't move, and Darcie couldn't. She lay there with Patrick bending over her, his hands curved around her shoulders, the smell of paint and the lyrical strains of

Puccini in the air.

'You're not hurt?' he growled, and she thought perhaps she should say yes, because instinct told her she would be safe if she claimed injury.

But she said, 'No,' and kept looking at his mouth as he was looking at hers, and there was no safety in that. None at all. On a great outrush of breath he lifted her to a sitting position, and her hands slipped all along the substantial curves of his arms, and her mouth met his with a sort of inevitability. He kissed her with great delicacy, with exquisite thoroughness. Slowly. Lighting the fuse and letting it burn. She was open-mouthed, out of breath when he drew back.

He stood up then, taking her with him. Looking deep in her eyes, he slipped the leather jacket from her shoulders, drew it down over her arms, then tossed it aside. When he took her in his arms again she was already half-way there. When he kissed her again she went up in flames, wild after the long years of fasting, released from the months of wariness where Patrick was concerned. She kissed him back, pushed her hands into his hair, feverishly touching him, exploring the substance of the broad back that she had once crazily thought to be lacking in aesthetic form. All the passion of her nature, stirred into life by him, was set free again, and she gave a little moan and twined her hands in his hair. Patrick bent and picked her up, and everything spun around her as he turned and lowered her on to a settee. Kneeling on the floor beside her, he unfastened her shirt and pushed it aside, his hands lingering on her soft, pale skin, tracing the pattern of her ribs, the full outer curves of her breasts, her shoulders. And Darcie explored him, too, delighting in the long, muscular line of arm and shoulder, the sculptural curves of his chest. His hands slipped down to her hips, and he bent to taste the valley between her breasts as he had once before.

'Oh, yes!' she gasped, her body arching into the sharp, sweet pleasure of Patrick's mouth on her breast. He moved to the other side and the piercing sensation went straight to the core of her, lifting her towards fulfilment, amazing her, shocking her.

'Darcie—you overwhelm me,' he said huskily, raising his head to see the look he'd put in her eyes. Darcie stared at him, holding her breath, scarcely able to believe the way she felt, the strength of her responses that she was, even now, deliberately blocking. *She* overwhelmed *him*? She was going up in smoke and he'd only touched her, caressed her. Her tongue ran over her suddenly dry lips. What would happen if they really made love—if she wrapped her legs around him and welcomed that beautiful, powerful body into hers? Her eyes closed for a moment as her body flared with anticipation, and the yearning was another long, astonishing pang of sensation.

Patrick sat on the edge of the settee and looked at her. 'Going too fast, sweetheart?' he said, and, when she didn't answer, he pulled the edges of her shirt together and went to pick up her jacket. Darcie fastened her buttons and tucked her shirt in, her embarrassment somehow smoothed away by Patrick's down-to-earth manner. He found a cloth and wiped the paint from her boots, then buffed a few spots of aubergine paint from the leather jacket and held it out for her. She slipped her arms in, her mind and body in a clamour as Patrick pulled her back against him.

'Are you serious about resigning?' he asked, dropping

a kiss on her neck that made her feel about ready to burst into flame again.

'More than ever!'

Patrick laughed. 'Well, then—when can I see you again?'

Darcie leapt away before her resolve burned to a cinder.

'You can't—I mean—not like that, not like this!'

'Not like what?'

'Can't see me again—not in that way, *this* way . . .'

'As lovers, you mean?'

She took a deep breath, aware that she sounded like a stammering high-school kid instead of a mature woman. 'Patrick—I—there's so much that's changing for me right now. A lot of it I have to thank you for, and I do thank you. The thing is,' she said, 'it's been a long time, and I'm not sure that I can handle—an affair. I loved Gavin, and I've stopped grieving, but I feel, I don't know—guilty about——' she waved her hand lamely, in the general direction of the couch '—this. It's too much for me—*you're too much for me*—you're too complex and I can't work out how I feel about you. Half the time I think I don't even like you, and the other half I—er——' Patrick raised his brows and she coloured. 'There are a lot of things I have to straighten out before I even think of complicating my life further . . .'

Patrick's mouth quirked. 'So, if I ask you to dinner, the answer's no?'

She felt injured by the flippancy, when she had been so painfully open. Drawing herself up, she said with dignity, 'I thought you, of all people, would appreciate honesty.'

He laughed shortly. 'It's just that there was so much

of it.' He found a doorpost and leaned a shoulder on it, assessing her with that academic air that masked whatever he was truly thinking. 'To tell you the truth, I'm not sure I'm any better equipped to handle an affair with *you*, sweetheart,' he said at last. 'I rather fancy a woman who's got it all together, not a mixed-up widow-woman who spends half her time worrying about a spotty teenager, and the other half involving me in scenes.'

Her relief was tempered with pique. She'd half expected him to be angry. After all, her fiery response had certainly led him a long way down the garden path, and here she was calling a halt.

'Matt isn't a spotty teenager. His acne has almost cleared up. Anyway, it's natural for a mother to worry over a son. Even a *step*mother.'

He smiled, slung an arm casually around her shoulder, and walked towards the door with her. 'Sure. I'm having a dig at you, that's all. Men get very irritable when the prospect of a night of love diminishes to a cold shower. Your maternal side is one of the things I like about you.'

'Oh,' she said, unsure that she found that flattering.

'You've no objection if we remain friends, I take it?' he asked, stooping to pick up her helmet. 'It would be more civilised, considering our business connections and my friendship with Matt.'

'Of course.' Darcie turned at the door to look seriously at him. She held out her hand to him, not even sure that was a good idea. Her heart was still bounding around. Before she could withdraw her hand, though, he had taken it. Thoughtfully, he turned it over and inspected her palm as if he might read something there that she hadn't told him. 'Reading all about you,' he'd said once. She curled her fingers over.

'You're right, you know. Sometimes the things you want just aren't a good idea.' His smile was warm and regretful, but philosophical.

It was all very adult and mature, she thought, kick-starting the bike. They both recognised the futility of getting involved with each other, and were smart enough to say so. She was too emotionally shaky to commit herself to a new relationship, and Patrick was looking for a different kind of woman. A less scrupulous man might have pursued the short-term benefits of an affair, and to hell with compatibility. Darcie admired his integrity. She congratulated herself on having the good sense to call a halt and the courage to speak her mind. She rode away, telling herself she should feel very pleased at having cleared the air, and wondering why she felt no overwhelming sense of satisfaction.

The next day she began checking through the Situations Vacant. She enquired about a job for a mechanic advertised at the local garage and, when the proprietor stopped laughing, promised to bring in her references. He hadn't seen the photo in the paper. Gary had, of course. He came over one evening to ask plaintively why she'd never told him about her past. But, from the wary way he regarded her, it was clear that he had decided they were not kindred spirits, after all. He left some vegetables with her and Darcie had a feeling that she had received her last lettuce.

Cut loose from her routine, with time for reflection, Darcie took a good look at herself and was disgusted. Once she had been disciplined and fit enough to climb mountains. Now she was out of breath carrying in the groceries. She bought herself a new track-suit and began jogging in the evenings; she went to a gym and worked

out. She had her hair reshaped and bought a new outfit
for Stephen James's christening the next month. On
impulse, she bought a totally impractical robe of flamingo
silk to replace her dressing-gown. A personal decision
entirely, she told herself, and nothing whatsoever to do
with Patrick's criticisms of her 'androgynous' nightwear.
He was around, as usual, to watch the golf on television
or to take Matt to his club, and his manner was easy and
friendly. Patrick, it seemed, was having a great deal less
trouble than she was in suppressing the odd chemistry
between them. Darcie was never able to subdue the small
flurry of excitement when she opened the door and found
him there. This was for the best, she told herself severely
whenever she found herself staring at him, remembering
how good it was to hold him and to be held. A headlong
affair was exactly what she did not need. Not yet. Maybe
never with Patrick.

But if it was friendship she wanted from him, then a
friend he turned out to be. Never more so than on Matt's
eighteenth birthday.

For Darcie, it was a strain. She might have travelled a
long way towards accepting his independence, but this,
his eighteenth birthday, demanded a final shift in her
mental state. The little boy, the touchingly mixed-up
youth, was gone. In the eyes of the world Matt was now a
man, and she couldn't help thinking of Gavin, who had
missed the last years of his son's childhood. All day she
was quite ridiculously close to tears.

They signed the contracts and celebrated Matt's
birthday in a restaurant with a group of his college and
racing friends. Mark, who had gone to Melbourne to
recuperate at his sister's home, sent his apologies, a
leather desk-set and six bottles of Bollinger. Darcie smiled

and laughed and proposed a toast to Matt, and felt as if she were breaking up inside. Just when she thought she might embarrass everyone by bursting into tears, Patrick removed her from her chair and took her to the dance-floor. There he pulled her close, shielding her from any watching eyes, and pressed a handkerchief into her hand. 'Let go, sweetheart,' he said in a low, low voice. 'It's OK to cry when your boy grows up.'

His understanding broke her, and she gulped and sobbed into his handkerchief as he gathered her in and laid his cheek against her hair and moved her slowly around the dance-floor.

'This is very thoughtful of you,' she said at last.

'The pleasure is all mine,' he murmured and, when she leaned back in surprise, he smiled and said, 'You've changed your hair.'

'Yes. Do you like it?'

He looked at it, touched it lightly, letting his hand come to rest across the back of her neck. The touch set off a chain reaction. Suddenly her body registered all the small, intimate contacts with him—his hand at her waist, the texture of his jacket beneath her palms, the brush of thigh on thigh.

'Yes,' Patrick said.

'Aren't you afraid all this fulsome flattery will go to my head?' she said, tongue in cheek.

He chuckled, and the vibrations of his laughter were another pleasure. 'Found a job yet?' he asked, after a while.

'I started work the day before yesterday. As a mechanic at the local garage,' she told him, pleased at the gleam of surprise in his eyes. 'Harry—the owner—thought I was pulling his leg when I first applied. He's been putting petrol in my car for years and thought I was a nice, quiet, suburban lady who typed and took shorthand.'

Patrick snorted. 'Poor Harry.'

Darcie was silent for a while, thinking of the difficulties of adjusting to the work again, the vaguely hostile humour of the two male mechanics which was still to be overcome, the discomfort of being regarded as a celebrity by certain customers who remembered her racing years. 'Harry sponsors a friend of his who's into racing—he gives Kev workshop time after hours and on weekends so that he can work on the car, and goes along to meetings as his back-up team. A lot of garages are involved with racing that way.'

Patrick drew back a little to look speculatively at her. He said nothing, just waited.

'Kev's hurt his ankle. It's in plaster and he's looking for a driver until he's fit again. He has the car entered in a couple of races and——' She shrugged. 'Naturally, they've asked me to drive the next race.'

'Thinking about making a comeback, Darcie?' he asked softly, and she looked over his shoulder, biting her lip. People kept asking her that, people who had tracked her down again since the article in the newspaper. Old friends like James Fitzgibbon, a driver and an old boyfriend, who said he could get her a drive in a Nissan at Amaroo. She'd heard from an old contact in advertising, from a biographer who wanted to talk to her about another book on Gavin, from an agent who had offered her film stunt work after Gavin's death, but had lost touch with her. They all assumed she was on the comeback trail—couldn't see any reason why she wouldn't be.

'Comeback might be too strong a word. I—might do a

few practice laps, to work some of the gremlins out of the car for Harry and Kev.' She had intended it to sound casual. Instead, it came out tentatively, revealing her apprehension, if not the extent of it. Patrick held her just a fraction closer, his hand clasped hers more firmly.

'You're scared.'

'To death. I must be a coward,' she said laughing shakily, tempted to tell him just how deep her fear went, and that surprised her because she'd never told anyone that. Not even Gavin.

'We'll see.'

Darcie clicked her tongue in exasperation. 'Most people would say, "Don't be silly, Darcie, of course you're not a coward" or "You've got nothing to prove".'

'Is that what you want me to say?'

Darcie was backed into a corner, aware that her annoyance was based on pettiness. In truth, what she had wanted from him, she realised now, was a word of praise, of encouragement. Because he was so sparing with them, they were somehow more valuable from Patrick. She sighed.

'You never say pretty words, do you—kind little white lies? You always tell the truth, the whole truth and nothing but the truth, don't you?'

Patrick looked down at her quizzically. 'Ninety-nine per cent of the time.'

'What about the other one per cent? What do you say when you're not being brutally honest?'

'Nothing,' he said. 'No comment at all is occasionally kinder than the truth.'

'No little white lies at all?' she mocked. 'You must be a wow with women. Did Theresa like that?'

His smile broadened. 'No comment,' he said, and, as

the band changed up to rock and roll, he whirled her around and showed her how light on his feet a big man could be. He was a good dancer, inventive and uninhibited, and Darcie spun away from him and dizzily back into his arms. She had gone on to the dance-floor in tears, but left it laughing.

'Thank you, Patrick,' she said, giving him back his handkerchief.

'Don't mention it. That's what friends are for.'

As a friend he was there the following Saturday when she ventured on to the track at Oran Park for a practice spin in Kev's Ford. James Fitzgibbon was there, too, and Patrick arrived in time to see Fitz greet her with all his former showy enthusiasm. He hugged her, lifted her off the ground, planted a kiss on both her cheeks and one on her mouth. 'Darling Darcie. I phoned everyone trying to track you down. Thought you'd buried yourself twelve thousand miles away in some little Cotswold village and eventually gave up. Never had such a shock when I saw your picture in the paper. Have dinner with me tonight. It'll be like old times. I won't take no for an answer.'

He flashed his incredible white smile at her and Darcie felt nineteen again, the age she'd been when first she met and fell rather heavily for Fitz's looks and charm. He hadn't changed much. He was tall and slim, and his almost too-pretty looks had benefited from the smile lines around his eyes and the frosting of grey in his black curly hair. Within minutes he was leaning with her into the engine of Kev's Ford, asking what work they'd done on it and how many revs they got and, in between, filling her in on old racing friends and their latest cars. It was like rolling back time, and Darcie talked and listened with the relish of someone who has not spoken or heard her own language for years. She laughed, buffed Fitz affectionately on the arm, and only then turned around to see Patrick.

Her quick surge of pleasure was somewhat dampened by his guarded smile. 'I expected to find you a bundle of nerves,' he said, glancing beyond her to Fitz.

'I am. Meeting Fitz again distracted me temporarily,' she said. Fitz came up then, and she introduced the two men, wondering if she imagined a certain wariness in the conversation that followed. They were still talking when she took a deep breath and got into Kev's car, they were talking four laps later when she headed up pit lane and told Kev and Harry that the new race engine wasn't giving the revs in top gear.

The men clustered around the car like surgeons around a patient. 'Could be the carburettor,' Darcie said.

Fitz nodded. 'Blocked jet. Could be.'

She was too absorbed in finding the flaw to dwell on her first venture for years on to a racetrack. When Patrick spoke to her again, she was happily covered in grease and quite calm.

'Why don't I take you to dinner tonight?' he said idly. 'Matt too, of course, if he's free.'

'Thanks, but I can't. I'm having dinner with Fitz.'

His eyes shifted to the other man, and narrowed. 'Is that so?' He looked irritated at the idea. Darcie watched his profile closely, wondering, almost hoping to find signs of jealousy there. But when he turned to her she received the usual mixed bag of signals. 'Watch your step.'

'What does that mean?'

He took her arm and moved her further away from the car and the men consulting over it. 'Your old boyfriend has a smooth manner and all the nostalgic appeal of the past. And right now you're very—susceptible.'

'Susceptible? To what?'

'You're a big girl. What do you think?'

Darcie put her hands on her hips. 'Are you insinuating that he has only to whisper a few reminiscent nothings in my ear for me to fall into bed with him?'

'You almost did with me,' he pointed out flatly. 'You're a passionate woman, long overdue for some loving. I—wouldn't want to see you get hurt.'

'Stop talking about me as if I'm a piece of ripe fruit to be plucked!' she said, flushing. 'I'm not totally without discrimination, even if I *did* act like a fool with you!'

'Yes, you did act like a fool with me, and I'm not even your type, as you've pointed out. He, on the other hand, is a driver with the aura of success, probably very glib with the kind little lies you like, and he looks not unlike Gavin. Many a widow has fallen for a less attractive substitute for a lost husband——'

'Well, what's it to you?' she demanded, annoyed by his practical air. 'Why don't you go look for your ideal, got-it-together, doormat-style playmate, instead of sticking your nose into my affairs—my life?'

His hands closed around her upper arms, and she was lifted on to her toes. 'Because,' he said between his teeth, 'although you drive me crazy, I don't want to see you fall flat on your face just as you're getting your confidence back. I don't want to see you expend all that—saved-up passion on a man who might take advantage of you.' His eyes roamed her face fiercely, then dropped to her mouth. 'I'm beginning to regret this "just friends" thing,' he growled.

Darcie's breath shortened. 'Are you?'

'If you've decided you're ready to pick up life again,' he said, his fingers flexing gently on her arms, 'you'd be a damned sight safer doing it with me.'

Safer with him? Had she not been so angry, she would have laughed. 'When I'm ready to "pick up life again", as you put it, Patrick, I'll be looking for more than a frolic with a safety net. Much more.' She glared. 'In any case, my love-life—or lack of it—is not open to discussion.'

Patrick sank his hands into his pockets and regarded her with his guarded, academic expression. 'Just keep your head where Fitzgibbon is concerned. Accept that as good advice from—a friend.'

Unnecessary advice, if he could but know. Everything he said was true—Fitz was dynamite. He was experienced and sophisticated, he talked her language and he had all the powerful appeal of nostalgia; but she was in no danger of losing her head over him. And she had a disquieting feeling that it was because her head was already more than a little lost. She went to dinner more than once with Fitz, she went dancing with him, she kissed him on several occasions and was kissed very thoroughly, very expertly. It was fun and uncomplicated and she felt alive and young again, but none of her 'saved-up passion' spilled over on to Fitz as it had with Patrick. Her friend, Patrick.

He offered no more advice on the matter, although he was frequently at the house, and she rarely mentioned Fitz's name. Mark had given in gracefully and the new line was now being fine-tuned by the market research people. Ensigns' promotional campaign was taking shape, and Matt had several photo sessions and lengthy interviews with the advertising team. Patrick delivered a heap of Ensigns luggage, sports bags and handbags to the house, with the request that, from now on, she and Matt carry no other product in public.

'You mean I have to turf all my old handbags out?' Darcie complained.

'Absolutely,' he said. 'It's in the contract.'

'I don't remember anything about handbags.'

He flicked her cheek. 'Should have read the fine print, sweetheart. You've got grease in your ear, did you know?'

'I'm a mechanic,' she retorted. 'What do you expect?'

There was an easiness between them now, a certain camaraderie even, that was evidence of Darcie's renewing confidence. Yet the chemistry was there, an undercurrent of tension that spiced the most casual contact. In an odd way, Darcie thought, acknowledging their physical attraction for each other and choosing to sublimate it had strengthened their friendship. It had certainly made it unique. Darcie had never had a friend like Patrick.

She went with him to choose his rose-bushes when his house renovations were nearing completion. They bought two pink Princess Margaret rose-bushes, white and red roses, hybrid teas, a trellised old-fashioned yellow rambler, and huge tubs to plant them in. 'Don't mention it,' she said when he thanked her. 'That's what friends are for.' It was beginning to sound like a theme song, she thought.

At his request, she also went with him to buy some new shirts. She thought about refusing such a cosy, domestic expedition, but the heady prospect of turning him out in some decent clothes proved too much for her. In the shops she inveigled him into trying on a grey double-breasted suit when he looked longingly at a ghastly brown one, its fabric shot with a greenish tinge. 'Not brown, Patrick. Surveys suggest that people don't trust businessmen in brown suits, did you know that?'

Patrick said he'd heard the theory, but never thought

much of it—however, if she thought there was
something to it . . . When he emerged from the
changing-room, looking powerful and distinguished in
the double-breasted grey, he met her eyes in the mirror
and gave a self-deprecatory grin. 'Trustworthy?'

'Very,' she said. She could hardly believe there'd been
a time when she didn't trust him.

They bought business shirts—neat blue and white
stripes and plain blue-grey. They bought silk ties in
muted shades to match the shirts—although Patrick
looked longingly at a peacock-blue affair—and they
bought a black dinner jacket and a plain white formal
shirt with tucks, although Patrick wistfully fingered a
black and white striped number with diamanté buttons
and frills.

'You'd look like a circus ringmaster in that,' she told
him, and he looked so meek that she regarded him with
suspicion for a moment. He had seemed mightily
amused all morning, come to think of it. 'What is
amusing you, Patrick?'

'You,' he said, smiling down at her. 'I've never been
on the receiving end of so much maternalism.'

Darcie bridled. Maternalism again. It wasn't fair that
such a lovely word carried with it images of brown cows
peacefully chewing the cud in a paddock. 'I don't feel in
the least maternal where you're concerned,' she said
waspishly. 'I'm simply doing you a favour, as a friend.'

'How can I thank you?' he murmured, and his eyes
were full of laughter as if he listened to some secret joke.

But he wasn't laughing a week later when he called at
Harry's garage. She was in the pit under the hoist,
working on the brakes of a Holden at the time, her
overalls in a state, her hands and face smeared with

grease. Her first indication that he was there was a kind of awareness of someone watching, a tingle along the spine. She peered past the car's underside and saw two large beautifully shod feet just above eye-level, and her heart gave a couple of heavy thuds. The knife-sharp creases of grey trousers crumpled as two long legs crouched down. A double-breasted grey jacket slid into view. A tasteful silk tie swung down, backed by a pale blue shirtfront, and Darcie, admiring all this sartorial splendour, gave a sigh of satisfaction.

'You're wearing your new suit.' She beamed as his shoulders thrust aggressively into view like a battering ram, followed by his face. 'You look——'

Terrific, she'd been going to say, but a cool breeze blew in from somewhere and she saw that his eyes were hard and remote and as cold as ice.

'I want to talk to you,' he said abruptly.

'I finish work in fifteen minutes——'

'Take a break. I've fixed it with Harry.'

She threw the hydraulic switch and raised the car, scrambled from the pit beneath it, and wiped her hands on the piece of cloth she kept dangling from her overalls pocket. 'I'm not crazy about you and Harry negotiating my teabreaks,' she told him. 'What do you want to talk to me about?' He looked so severe that she grew anxious. 'There's nothing wrong with Matt, is there?'

'No, it's OK, it's not Matt.' He took her arm and walked her without comment through the lunch-room adorned with the girly calendars of the motor trade, to the privacy of the garage's unlovely back entrance, where he unfurled the newspaper to display the social pages.

'This is what it's about,' he said, and indicated a

photograph of Darcie with James Fitzgibbon, the two of
them laughing in a nightclub setting.

'Darcie Brooke, better known as Darcie Miller,
former racing star, and James Fitzgibbon, veteran
driver with the Bamstead-backed Nissan team, talking
over old times. Ms Miller, widow of Grand Prix
driver Gavin Brooke, is soon to see her stepson, Matt
Brooke, embark on a racing career, and says she is
considering Fitzgibbon's offer to team up with him
once again for the Wynn's Safari Marathon next year.
They won the event seven years ago.'

'You didn't tell me that Fitzgibbon had asked you to
co-drive with him.'

Her temper stirred. 'It might come as a surprise,
Patrick, but I don't tell you every little thing.'

'You're seeing a lot of him,' he said, eyes narrowed.
'How serious is it? Maybe you're already co-driving?'

She drew in her breath sharply at the offensiveness of
it.

'You won't, of course, be co-driving in any rallies with
him,' he went on. 'Neither will you accept any drives he
offers you. And, in future, you won't be photographed
with him.'

'Is that so?' she exclaimed. 'Watch it, Patrick, I'll be
thinking you're *jealous*!'

His mouth tightened, denting in whitely at each
corner, and Darcie felt a primitive little flare of delight.

'This is official, Darcie. Ensigns isn't backing Matt
only to have his name associated, however indirectly,
through you, with another driver and, particularly,
another sponsor.' He slapped the picture and caption
with the back of one hand. 'This is a tidy bit of

advertising for Fitzgibbon's sponsor. You've given Bamstead the lustre of both the Brooke name *and* that of Darcie Miller, all for nothing, and Ensigns doesn't even get a mention!'

Jealous! What an idiot she was to let such a thought cross her mind. All this cold anger was purely business orientated. Darcie marched away. 'So sue me!' she said over her shoulder.

'I hope it won't come to that.'

Darcie turned back to him. 'Sue me? Patrick—you wouldn't!' There was an injured note in her voice, and a trace of anxiety. Patrick's eyes flickered a bit.

'You signed an undertaking not to use your name or reputation in any way detrimental to Ensigns' agreement with Matt. I consider linking your name, and therefore Matt's, with a Bamstead-sponsored driver to be detrimental.'

She gaped at him, remembering the clause and her lack of interest in it. At the time she hadn't envisaged ever being involved in driving again, but things had changed. Her brain ran the dry legal phrases through for review, and her eyes opened wide. Any move she made towards reviving her own career could, because of the close association of the Miller and Brooke names, be construed as having an effect on Matt's, if someone wanted to be legally picky about it. And Patrick did, apparently. In effect, he could control almost anything she did. The blood rushed to her face.

'You pig!' she said, 'No wonder you pushed me into that publicity about Mark. No wonder you wanted me to drive again. Like a fool, I'd begun to think you were encouraging me just because you liked me.'

'I do like you,' he said.

'If this is liking, I hope you never *dis*like me!' she snapped. 'You'll block anything I want to do on the grounds that it doesn't enhance Ensigns' publicity, so, in effect, you've got *me* under contract, too! And I have no excuse. I've been bitten in the past and I should have known better. Damn you, Patrick!'

She was so hurt, so disappointed, that she lashed out at him with her cleaning rag. It left a long black grease smear across his beautiful double-breasted suit, she saw, before she stormed away and left him standing.

CHAPTER SEVEN

ON THE Thursday before Stephen James's christening, Darcie collected her air ticket, and wrapped the gift she'd bought. On Friday night she packed her bag, and on Saturday morning airport technicians went on strike. All passengers booked on weekend flights were advised to make other arrangements. Darcie made frantic phone calls. No, madam, no Saturday flights at all. But, madam, your ticket is fully refundable. Sorry, madam, for any inconvenience.

Inconvenience! Her parents were in Mackay; Matt, who had driven up with a mate two days earlier, was in Mackay—even her brother had made it there from Canberra. Her godson was being christened amid a rare family reunion, and she was stranded one thousand, three hundred miles away in Sydney!

She considered driving, thought of the elderly Toyota and the work it would need to sustain it for such a long trip, and abandoned the idea. Passenger coach? Certainly, madam, the bus leaves Sydney this afternoon, and arrives at Mackay at ten-past midnight on Monday. 'But the christening's at ten on Sunday morning!' she wailed. Very sorry, madam. What about a train? No trains until tonight. Too late, too slow.

'Oh, blast!' she exploded when the doorbell sounded. She flung the door open, almost welcoming the chance to vent her frustration on a pushy salesman. Her scowl-

126

ing gaze fell on a big left shoulder. Patrick leaned nonchalantly beside the door, looking out at her front garden full of pitiful-looking pruned roses. He turned to her, and for a moment, as only the left side of his face was visible, she received a blast of such warmth that her heart thumped in her chest. But then he was facing her fully, and the warmth was weakened by that cool, guarded, calculating right side.

'Matt's not here. He and a friend drove up north two days ago,' she said coolly. It was the first time she'd seen him since the day he'd come to the garage, and her disappointment was too deep for forgiveness yet. 'His friend is visiting family in Sarina, and Matt will stay with my brother.'

'For the christening. I know,' he said, studying her cream boots, her red jump-suit and her side-pinned hair with that academic approval she disliked. 'All dressed up and nowhere to go, Darcie?'

'It's not funny!' she snapped. 'I'm the *godmother* and I'm not going to be there!'

He grinned, and there was a pleased, boyish air about him, as if he was about to produce a rabbit from a hat.

'Get yourself a warm jacket, godmother. You *shall* go to the christening.'

She blinked, then looked past him at his BMW parked in the street. Hope bloomed. If she drove all night she could probably make it in a BMW. 'You're going to let me have your car?'

'I'm going to let you have *me*,' he said, and as he walked inside she realised that he was wearing his leather flying jacket.

They flew into Mackay in a chartered Piper Cherokee that afternoon, over emerald-green sugar-cane country, into the warm winter weather of the tropics and a warmer welcome from the gathered Millers. Darcie ran into her parents' double embrace, was hugged and kissed and anxiously checked over for weight loss and bags under the eyes, then released to her older brother, Greg, who whirled her off the ground, kissed her twice, and passed her to Martin for more of the same. Matt was out riding, and Stephen James was asleep at home with Sara, her brother told her.

'Wait till you see him!' he said with a grin.

The immediate babble died and everyone turned to Patrick, the outsider in this tight group. Darcie introduced him, conscious of intense speculation on the part of her mother, who openly reviewed his craggy, unhandsome face and big solid figure in the faded jeans and battered flying jacket. 'A good friend of mine,' she'd described him on the phone when her mother wanted to know just who *was* this sainted pilot who was bringing her to them in the face of the worst-timed strike in history? In spite of his disappointing warnings and threats the other day, he remained a good friend. Unasked, Patrick had come to help her when she needed it because he cared that she might miss something so important to her. Her gratitude swelled to include a whole lot more, but she let only the gratitude show as her mother cast one of her fact-finding glances over her.

'How do you do, Mrs Miller,' Patrick said, holding out his hand. Darcie smiled wryly as he found himself enveloped in her family's enthusiasm. 'Patrick, you're a saint,' her father quipped, pumping his offered hand several times. 'Bringing Darcie to us like this.' Eva Miller, disdaining anything so formal as a handshake, grasped his arms and hauled her diminutive height upwards to kiss him on the cheek. 'Oh, dear,' she said, measuring his height anxiously, 'I hope the bed we've prepared for you will be long enough.' Greg and Martin repeated the hand-pumping and said that any friend of Darcie's was a friend of theirs. Patrick's startled gaze met Darcie's. He seemed quite disorientated, she thought in amusement, watching him fall in step with her mother. Eva Miller was asking questions and shooting intent, appraising looks up at Patrick, and Darcie, following arm-in-arm with her father, would have given a lot to know what she was saying.

Martin's home was a modest old timber house set on several acres. Sugar-cane grew up against one of his boundaries, chickens and ducks pecked around in an enclosure, and a great, lolloping, slobbery dog raced around welcoming the new arrivals.

There was another welcome from Matt and Sara, and, eventually a hushed moment when Stephen James was put into Darcie's arms. For a long time she stared into the face of the tiny baby and was lost for words. The feel of him, the soft baby smell of him, touched her as she'd never been touched before. He screwed up his face and, carefully, she transferred him to her shoulder where he gave vent to an enormous burp.

'Should I take that as approval, Sara?' she laughed, looking around. But Sara wasn't there. No one was there. Only Patrick, watching her with a most odd expression in his eyes.

'How come you and Gavin didn't have children?'

'We travelled a lot. Gavin liked us with him when he raced, so we were like nomads. We were waiting until he retired to start a family.' The baby's fist closed around her index finger, as if to emphasise all that she'd missed. 'I always planned on having at least four children.'

'And will you?'

She gave him an old-fashioned look. 'I'm twenty-seven. Time's against me.'

'So old!' he mocked. 'Don't give up. Two sets of twins and you could have your nursery full by the time you're thirty.'

'How very practical,' she said drily, 'but there aren't any twins in my family.'

'Find a man with some in his.'

She looked up quickly. Patrick was a twin. He smiled at her, looking half teasing and half serious. But he always looked half serious. She wasn't his type, she reminded herself. He wanted a serene, fully realised woman without complications. To her he wanted to be a friend, and he was. Keep it light, she told herself. 'Ah, but is that a guaranteed solution? Don't twins skip a generation every now and then?' she said in mock earnestness.

'It happens,' he admitted. 'It would be a calculated risk.'

'Oh, I've taken calculated risks before. The problem is, where would I find this answer to my every need? He'd have to be a fine, upstanding figure of a man if he was going to be father to my children. I wouldn't want a wimp. He'd have to be—er . . .'

'Fertile,' he said, dead-pan.

'Oh, absolutely. Fertile, with a history of multiple births in his family. And he'd have to be able to sing on key.'

'Sing?' he repeated, blinking. 'You did say, *sing*?'

Darcie looked at him in mock seriousness. 'Well, I *can't*, you see. Sing in tune, I mean. Hopelessly tone-deaf. And did you know that if a tone-deaf mother sings to her children, there's a good chance they'll grow up tone-deaf too?'

Patrick said gravely that he didn't know that.

'So you see, *someone* has to sing to the kids—you can't have children growing up without singing.'

'Perish the thought. Maybe you should look around in opera circles for a fertile, well-built tenor——'

'Or a baritone,' she said tolerantly. 'The quality of the voice isn't important, only the tunefulness. But I'd have to love him, of course, and vice versa, otherwise the deal would be off—even if he was a triplet with a voice like Pavarotti.'

'That's a tall order.'

'No taller than yours,' she pointed out with malicious sweetness. 'Where are you going to find this warm, stable, self-realised, *passionate* doormat you want?'

He folded his arms across his chest. 'I've got more chance of success than you,' he said.

'How do you figure that out?'

'Mine doesn't have to sing.'

There were suspiciously frequent occasions during the weekend when Darcie found herself alone with Patrick. After dinner that night, for instance, when everyone but Sara and Martin went for a walk. Within a very short time, Greg, Matt and her parents were way behind, leaving Darcie and Patrick walking together in the moonlight with only the lolloping great dog for company. Darcie was conscious of the space between them, the light touch of the breeze on her face, the indigo sky with its seemingly patternless scatter of stars. But there *was* a pattern, she thought. The breeze was part of it, and the stars. Maybe even the space between her and Patrick.

The dog crashed around in the long grass by the road, his breath a steady, rhythmic panting. 'Buster—here, Buster!' she called him as he galloped off beside the sugar-train tracks that crossed the road.

'He's probably hoping to find a snake,' Patrick said.

'A snake!' Darcie's muscles contracted in conditioned response and she tripped on the train track.

Patrick caught her before she fell, scooping her up against his chest. 'The cane-fields are full of them. You don't like snakes?'

She shook her head. 'But lizards are worse. I hate lizards. It's those little legs . . .' Her voice croaked out. Patrick's hands spread warmly on her back, a gentle pressure that kept her close against him. She held on to his shoulders and thought that *now* the pattern of the night was perfect. The breeze, the stars in their place. She in hers. Patrick tightened his arms around her, tilting his head as if he might kiss her. The chemistry was as potent as ever. If he kissed her she might not be able to stop, and her parents were strolling around the corner even now.

'No!' she said, making it more urgent because she didn't want to say it at all. 'Let me go.'

He stiffened, eyes glittering. Sardonically he murmured, 'Don't panic. It's the dog you can hear panting.'

'I didn't mean—that is, the others aren't far behind us and I don't want them getting the wrong idea and thinking that we're—er——'

'Lovers,' he said baldly. 'Perish the thought. We don't want your mother lying awake listening for the sound of creaking floorboards in the night.'

They walked on with a space between them, and Darcie sighed for the patterns of a perfect night.

'Mum, I hope you haven't got the wrong idea about Patrick and me,' she said before breakfast the next morning.

'Oh, goodness, no. I'm sure I haven't,' her mother said with a reassuring smile, and total lack of guile in her blue eyes. 'He's just a friend, you told us that. Not that it isn't time you were considering something more. You tied yourself up in knots after Gavin died and wouldn't let us help you, and we wondered if you'd work it out. Some things you have to work out for yourself. Like getting used to the idea of Matt getting into racing. I know that's hard.'

'You don't know the half of it, Mum,' she sighed.

'Don't I?' Eva said drily, transferring bacon to the grill. 'I always knew he might take it up, and yet I—I can't believe it—I just—blinded myself to it. I was so *sure* he was going to be an accountant. I used to picture him in a suit, in a nice safe office in the city.'

'Oh, yes,' her mother nodded. 'For me it was a dress-maker.'

Darcie wrinkled her nose and laughed. 'What?'

'I used to picture you sitting serenely at a sewing-machine, making things with frills on them.' She gazed out of the window, a rasher of bacon dangling from the fork in her hand. 'The frills were very important. Symbolic, I suppose, of a very feminine occupation. It helped me sleep at night. But,' she sighed, slapping the rasher on the grill, 'I suppose deep down I always knew you'd go and race cars. Mothers are funny creatures.'

'But,' Darcie stared at her mother, 'you never let on. You never panicked about the danger, or tried to talk me out of driving.'

'Inside I did. But I had to come to terms with it. It was

your dream, love. Surest way to lose someone is to stomp on their dreams.'

'Yes. Patrick said that once——'

'Did he?' She nodded in approval. 'Anyway, I can tell you now, it was a glad day for me when you retired from it.'

Darcie didn't have the heart to mention Kev's car and the practice sessions. It hardly constituted a comeback, after all. Let her mother sleep easy. She set the breakfast-table while Eva asked some pointed questions about Patrick.

'I don't like that look in your eye, Mum.'

'What look is that, love?' Eva asked, and turned a very shrewd, approving look on Patrick as he came in for breakfast.

'That's the one,' Darcie muttered.

Bacon grilled, eggs fried, bread toasted, coffee brewed. It was all consumed, cameras checked, and car-seating arrangements for the christening finalised. And when the bustle of washing-up had finished, everyone found absorbing chores elsewhere and Darcie found herself strolling along Martin's three-acre block with Patrick. Her mother's stage management was simply superb, she acknowledged wryly.

A cousin of last night's breeze teased the fields of sugar-cane that bounded the property's south side, dipping like an invisible finger into the lush, emerald mass and running across the crop's surface. Martin and Sara's chickens clucked in soft contentment, palm fronds rattled, and Buster galloped in circles, yipping his pleasure. Some early cloud was breaking up, leaving the sky a fine, pale blue.

'What a beautiful sky!' Darcie laughed.

'Mmm,' Patrick said, squinting at it, 'I've got an old faded pair of jeans that colour.'

'How poetic.'

'Accurate,' he grinned. 'I'll show you some time.'

Patrick tossed a stick and Buster went tearing after it.

'This reminds me of home, when we were kids,' Darcie said, watching the dog retrieve the twig in slobbery jaws. 'Mum and Dad's place was a bit like this, only bigger, because Dad farmed. We had a creek to swim in and a hill to race billy-carts down and tractors that we all learned to drive before we were teenagers.'

'You had a lot of space to grow up in. I envy you.'

'You must have had grander homes than mine.'

'Grander, maybe. We used to spend months every year at a country house, but in between we always lived in inner-city apartments. It suited my parents' life-style.'

'I suppose you had parks to play in. That wouldn't have been so bad.'

'Oh, sure, the apartments always had a kids' playground, but I remember at one place we were on the twenty first floor I could see another park from my window, and that was the one I wanted to go to. It had a roundabout, you see.' He crinkled up his eyes reminiscently. 'I really wanted to ride on that roundabout.'

She gave a little crow of triumph. 'I *thought* you looked sheepish when I caught you with one foot on the one by the river.'

'Nothing of the kind,' he said equably. 'I was just fooling around, giving you time to compose yourself. Anyway, I conned the kid downstairs into loaning me his bike a few times, and I rode around the streets for hours, but never did find that park. I dare say it was further away than it looked from the twenty-first floor,' he said with a wry sort of smile.

'How old were you?'

'Six.'

Six. She had a mental picture of him at six, pedalling around on a bike too big for him, determined to find the park he'd seen and wanted from his window. If ever Patrick found the woman he wanted, she wouldn't have a chance of escaping. But then, she thought, would a woman wanted by Patrick think of escape?

Stephen James was tranquil until the last moments of his christening ceremony, when he let loose with a protesting yell. Darcie made her responses as godmother, and fleetingly wondered if this might be her lot in life. Always the godmother, never the mother? she joked to herself. There was the photo session, and later the gifts to be opened, and a celebration lunch attended by a small army of friends as well as the family. Matt's friend cruised by in his Celica and picked him up. They were taking a day trip over to Brampton Island before they returned to Sydney, they said. When it was time for Darcie and Patrick to leave there was another round of hugs and kisses 'until the next time'. Darcie smiled and waved to her family as she walked with Patrick to the plane, valiantly concealing the ridiculous emotion that welled up inside her. At least, she thought she was concealing it. When they had taken off and were high above the cane-fields, Patrick passed her a handkerchief without comment. And, without comment, she cried into it.

Perhaps it was that unspoken understanding that broke down the last barrier she had against Patrick, perhaps it was the cumulative effect of being with him in the loving glow of her family. And perhaps it was simply the knowledge that there was nothing she could not tell him.

'The last time I drove professionally,' Darcie heard herself say, 'I—was forced out of the race because I lost a wheel. But I expect you know that—it's in the files. One of my wheels came off and everyone said what rotten luck.' He turned his head and she said in a rush, 'You asked about my last race once, so I'm telling you.'

Apparently he saw nothing odd about this belated answer to the question he'd asked her so long ago. He just nodded.

'I let them think that,' she said, clearing her throat. 'Just a faulty wheel and rotten luck. But in fact——'

'In fact you went blank,' he said softly. 'Lost it.'

'I don't know what happened. It was as if I'd forgotten everything I knew, even the most elementary driving skills. The car got away from me and spun into a crowd barrier.' Perspiration filmed her forehead and top lip. She paused to wipe it away. 'Of course, the barrier was built to withstand impact, and it held and no one was hurt. My wheel came off and flew through the air, over the barrier, and still no one was hurt. But I saw it, Patrick—I sat there frozen and saw it pass so close to a little girl who was perched on her father's shoulders. I thought at first it had hit her. Her name was Deborah McDonald, and she told me it touched her hair as it passed. A fraction more to one side and I could have killed Deborah McDonald.' She stared down at the green, gold and mauve tapestry of the earth below. 'She was five.'

Vaguely she wondered if he would say 'the wheel would have come off whether you blanked out or not', or 'what idiot of a father puts a kid on his shoulders at a racetrack barrier, anyway?', in an attempt to exonerate her, as she had initially tried to exonerate herself. But, of course, he didn't. He was Patrick.

'And you didn't race again?'

'If I hadn't gone blank like that, I wouldn't have spun in that spot, and the wheel wouldn't have bounced over the barrier into the crowd.' She shrugged. 'No one else thought anything of it. Near misses happen all the time in racing, but I couldn't get it out of my head that I could have killed Deborah. I should have forced myself to get back in the car, but I didn't. I lied and said I'd hurt my neck. But the headaches I started getting were real enough. It was almost the end of the season and I cancelled my remaining drives.'

'Yes, I see.'

'Gavin and I were married a few months after the accident, and he didn't want me to go back to racing. He was quoted as saying there wasn't room in a marriage for two drivers, and I went along with it, even believed that because it suited me to believe it. Even Gavin didn't know that I'd jumped at the excuse he gave me to retire. That way I wouldn't have to admit I was too scared to drive again.' She sighed. 'Then, later, there was Matt. I wanted to keep him away from racing, that was true, but he gave me a legitimate reason to turn my back on everything that made me feel so bad. All this time I've been busy hating everyone connected with the sport, cutting myself off from old friends . . . when it was really myself I hated for letting fans believe I was some kind of hero, sacrificing my career for my husband's, for not having the guts to admit I couldn't do it any more because I was just plain scared.' She leaned back, tired suddenly, yet conscious of a weight gone from her. 'You *said* I'd tell you everything eventually,' she said with a shaky laugh.

'And is that everything?' he asked.

'I always imagined that I'd retire one day and have a special cabinet built for my trophies. Something to look back on—be proud of—remind me that I was good.' Patrick looked at her and she gave a wry smile. 'My trophies are in a packing-case at home, wrapped in tissue paper.' She was silent for a long time as she looked down at the earth made more beautiful by distance. From up here, she thought, rivers looked tranquil and tame, manmade ugliness was absorbed into the colours of nature. From up here it looked as if the mountains were small enough to move.

'I'll drive Kev's car in that race next month.' The words and the intention hung there, intimidating her. She gave a nervous little camouflage laugh, which didn't work. 'Subject to your approval. I wouldn't want to endanger Matt's contract with Ensigns.'

Patrick took her hand, held it strongly, and she felt better. Then he raised it, and kissed it in a courtly, tender gesture that made her catch her breath. He looked at her strangely, as if he was searching for words, and it was a few moments before he said, in a low, rough tone, 'You're special, Darcie Miller. You're loving and compassionate and gutsy and I——' he stopped, blinked rapidly '—I thank you for telling me.'

Darcie wasn't quite sure why she was disappointed with that. Some vague feeling he'd been going to say something else. Or some vague wish. Take it easy, Darcie, she thought, smiling at Patrick and telling herself to appreciate what she had here. He could have been her lover and it could all be over by now, and any chance of lasting friendship with it. This had depth and warmth and an enduring quality, and she valued it. And if that other part of her that Patrick had stirred was not satisfied with it, then it was too bad. Life was offering a great deal and she must not be greedy. One comeback at a time, she told herself. One comeback at a time.

CHAPTER EIGHT

WAITING at the starting line for a race to begin could take twenty minutes, sometimes longer. A heart-thumping, palm-sweating time as the body prepared for the wrenching effort ahead and the mind came to terms yet again with the risks. Darcie had waited like this so often before, reviewing the practice performance of the car and its weaknesses, waiting for the cold objectivity that always came just seconds before the start signal.

She took a quick look at the other drivers on grid, matching their qualifying times with their reputations, and smiled ruefully at her own, which had earned her a place in the third row. To the old Darcie Miller, third would have been humiliating. The old Darcie Miller would have gritted her teeth and promised herself to wipe the cocky, malicious, chauvinistic grins off the face of several male drivers. But the old Darcie Miller had mellowed.

Her eyes flickered sideways, searching. It shouldn't be hard, she thought, to find a man built like a tank in a crowd. Matt was there, wearing a red cap with 'Ensigns' printed on it, and beside him was Mark. Darcie lifted her gloved hand to them. She couldn't see Patrick, but she could see barricades and people pressed close to them. A man with a little boy perched on his shoulders. Darcie felt sick.

The one-minute signal went up and her hands

clenched. Around her the engine noise reached a crescendo. Thirty seconds. Her nerves steadied, she stared through the ranks at the car in pole position and felt the old, familiar flare of envy whenever another driver was on pole instead of her. With the envy came a surge of desire to cut down his advantage and beat him. The old, competitive Darcie was mellowed, but not gone, she thought with a grin. The flag dropped, she released the clutch, her wheels spun. Into first gear and she was looking for a gap at the first corner.

The initial scrap broke up as the fastest qualifiers shot away, opening a gap to the next four cars. Darcie hung in, settling into the familiar rhythm, nosing up behind a Sierra and sticking there. He was a wily veteran and went into his corners taking the centre line to prevent her from passing inside. She waited, pressed across as if she intended an outside pass, and when he moved to block her there as well she plunged to the inside line and passed him. She felt cool, clear-headed. There was only the track ahead and the cars to chase and the fear to be kept in its place.

She pulled up to sixth position when another car burst a tyre on the S-bends and was out of the race in a cloud of dust. Fifth, when she went into a corner with the cockiest, most chauvinistic of her current competitors, and left him behind when he used his brakes too early, convinced that she would not have the nerve to stay off hers. From fifth to fourth. Lap fifteen of twenty-five. Her times were better, far better, than her qualifying times. Harry and Kev had scrawled large kisses with the time on her pit-board last time around.

Lap eighteen. Another competitor was out, both car and driver steaming but unhurt by the side of the track, and the oil flag was being shown to warn drivers that there had been a spill. Darcie aimed for the apex of a bend with another car crowding her for the inside. She was forced to run slightly wide and the thing she dreaded more than anything happened. The other car clipped her tail and tipped her into a spin.

It was a small, private world, soundless, lonely, But not so lonely as that last time when her brain had shut down and failed her. The world rushed past the windows in a blur, and Darcie perspired and stayed with it, working to bring the car to a stop, mindful of the nearness of the barrier to her side and the danger of being hit by one or more of the following cars. When she succeeded, she felt neither triumphant nor afraid. It was all part of the job, and this time her thinking-machine had not let her down.

The triumph came later. She had lost too much time and came in seventh.

'Tough luck,' Harry said.

'Sorry about the damage, Kev,' she said.

Kev was philosophical. 'All in the game. Not your fault, love. Shame, though. You had a chance until he clipped you.'

'Bad luck, Darcie,' a few people called.

'Would you call this a setback rather than a comeback, Darcie?' a reporter quipped.

'You did great,' from Matt, with a consoling pat on the back.

'But for that incident, you could have won,' from Mark.

But none of them knew that she *had* won, just by being here, just by finishing the race. Impatiently, Darcie looked for the one person who did know. She answered the reporter who was joined by another, she posed for a photograph and joked that she'd never had her picture taken for coming in seventh before, and all the time she looked for Patrick. At last she saw him, and her eyes shone and she was laughing and crying all at once and moving towards him, blindly brushing aside those who stood between them. His arms went around her, crushed her to him and she felt him trembling. Patrick, trembling. She held him tight.

'I was terrified at the start,' she said into his shirt.

'I know.' His voice was rough, uneven.

'I did lousy lap times at the end.'

'Practically standing still.'

'Only came seventh. Me, Darcie Miller, seventh!'

Patrick looked into her eyes and she almost burned up in the heat of his admiration. 'You're one hell of a woman,' he said, and his eyes smiled and made a winner of her. 'Congratulations, Darcie Miller.'

She laughed in elation. 'Aren't you going to kiss me? All racing drivers get kissed after a race.' He bent to her and she slipped her arms around his neck, and his mouth was tantalisingly close to hers when she was hauled backwards.

'Tough luck, honey!' Fitz yelled and got a grip on her waist to whirl her around. 'But you still take a corner as good as any man!'

His chauvinistic praise raised a smile from her, but she could have wished Fitz to the devil. As he bestowed several kisses on her she peered over his shoulder at Patrick. But he had turned away casually to talk to Mark, and the next time she looked she couldn't see him at all. The day suddenly fell a little flat.

The car was loaded on to the trailer. She went back to

the garage with it and spent a couple of hours going over the damage with Harry and Kev, reporting on the car's slight understeer, defining the weaknesses to be fixed for the next race. The two men ushered her out eventually, with winks and a sudden, puzzling joviality, and she went home to shower and change. Mark had invited her over for dinner and she dressed for it a little wistfully. She had been hoping to celebrate this day more fully. In the mirror she pulled a face at herself. With Patrick, was what she meant. But Patrick had not suggested any such celebration. Nor had Matt, though he did have a date with Roberta. For all she knew, Patrick might have a date, too. Terrific, she thought, hanging on stubbornly to the brightness of the day.

At Mark's house, a swarm of people leapt out from behind the antiques and shouted, 'Surprise!' Not a quiet dinner for two, after all, but a party to celebrate her comeback. His elegant house was bedecked with balloons and chequered flags. Fitz was there, and several other drivers with partners. Harry and Kev, of course, whose wives were already looking a little glazed at the endless race-talk. Matt was there with Roberta, who was drinking champagne and giggling rather a lot. Darcie took him aside to warn him not to let her drink any more.

'Yeah, yeah. This is your comeback party—can't you take a break from nagging?'

'It's a foul job, but someone has to do it,' she told him.

There was a festive cake in the shape of a car and, flanking it, some of her trophies which Matt had brought, tarnish and all, and there was a great sheaf of flowers from her parents with a card inscribed in her mother's hand with the plaintive message, 'Congratulations. Why couldn't you have been a dressmaker?'

And Patrick was there. She looked up from the flowers and saw him and her smile lit up. Before she could make it to his side, though, Harry grabbed her to resolve an argument over one of her previous races. Her protest that this was a party and their wives not interested in such technicalities was treated with hilarity. The conversation inexorably fixed on cars and racing and, short of being rude, Darcie was unable to escape.

'I locked up a gearbox over the hump and the wheel studs popped off . . .'

'. . . broke the accelerator cable. So what do you reckon, he hooked the accelerator cable up to the choke knob and pulled the choke in and out! I tell you . . .'

'. . . one tenth of a second slower than Brockie's 54.7, it was . . .'

'And I told them the tyre compound was for a colder track and, mate, this track was getting warmer by the minute . . .'

Escape. Darcie turned the word over as the champagne flowed and the race-talk grew nostalgic. Here she was with people who spoke her language, and she thought about escape. It never would have happened in the old days.

'. . . an oil adaptor block, would you believe, right between the oil pump and the spot where the standard filter screws on to the . . .'

Darcie was asked to describe her winning races, and she did. She was asked about Gavin, and the words came easily. She was asked what her plans were now.

'I think,' she said, smiling, holding one of her tarnished trophies, 'I'm going to have a special cabinet built for my trophies.'

She wanted to talk to Patrick, but in fact she talked to everyone *but* Patrick. An hour later she saw him slip away, and caught up with him in the garden, sitting on a low stone wall. The air was heavy with the night-fragrance of a Rondeletia, bowed with its burden of pink flowers. Patrick watched her coming towards him, his eyes crinkled against the drift of smoke from his cigar.

'I didn't know you smoked,' she said, watching the cigar tip glow as he inhaled.

'Once every blue moon.'

She sat down beside him and sipped from her champagne glass. Now that she had him alone, she wasn't sure where to start.

'I've been trying to get you alone all evening,' she blurted out.

Patrick turned to look down at her. 'Why's that?'

'To tell you I——' She stopped the words just in time. They had come without conscious intention, from the heart of her. To tell you I love you. To tell him that she had a powerful feeling that he loved her, too, but when it came to the point, she discovered she wasn't quite the daredevil she had once been, wasn't quite prepared to risk so much without some encouragement. One comeback at a time, Darcie. She had another swallow of champagne and smiled brightly at him. 'To tell you I'm grateful for all that you've done.' She cringed at the stiff formality. Patrick gave a twisted sort of smile. 'I might never have made it to this day without you, Patrick. If you hadn't needled me, made me face the truth, started me thinking, *really* thinking, about where I was going, I might never have found the courage to come back.'

'You would have. Matt would have had to come out in the open eventually.'

She shook her head. 'I could have lost him. All that brutal honesty of yours was just what I needed.'

He laughed. The cigar smoke made the sound husky, slightly dry. 'Was it?'

'Oh, I'm not saying I *liked* it much at the time. We don't always like what's good for us. I would have preferred pretty words, but they were bad for me then.' She smiled up at him. 'Have you any for me now, Patrick?'

His eyes flicked to the champagne glass, over her face, and beyond to Mark's beautiful, moonlit garden. 'I'm not sure I can make the transition,' he murmured, and he turned to her as if he would say more, but there was a burst of music and a few couples danced out on to the lawn. Fitz detached himself from the others and came over a trifle unsteadily, bearing a champagne bottle. 'Darcie, me darlin',' he cried with a mock Irish brogue, 'I've been looking for you.'

Patrick flicked ash from his cigar. 'Here come your pretty words,' he said sardonically.

Fitz caught her up and she gave a shriek as he whirled her off the ground. Champagne flew in a silver spray from her glass, and Darcie caught a glimpse of Patrick watching. The next time she looked, he wasn't there. He wasn't inside the house, either. Patrick, it transpired, had gone home. Her dismay was complete. The party went on around her and she wasn't truly there. Darcie was floating on air, her self-esteem restored, but Patrick had gone and left a gap that no celebration could fill. Within the hour, she slipped away and drove to his house.

The scaffolding had gone now. The exterior trims glowed a soft terracotta; the rubble had been cleared

away and transformed into a paved courtyard dotted
with the tubs of roses she'd helped him choose. As she
knocked at Patrick's door her heart was pounding faster
than it had when she had spun on an oily track. If he
asked why she was here, what would she say? That
being somewhere else without him wasn't her idea of
celebrating? That today she'd started taking risks again,
and this was one of them? Or would she have the
courage simply to say she was here because she loved
him? Even as the door opened, her courage waned.

Patrick stared at Darcie. He stepped outside to look past
her into the street, wondering if she'd brought a horde of
party guests with her. There was no one else. Darcie,
alone on his doorstep in the middle of the night. The
possibilities ranged themselves temptingly in his mind,
delivered a gigantic kick to his gut.

'What are you doing here, Darcie?' he asked. The
question came out rougher than he meant.

She hesitated a moment, and those revealing blue eyes
of hers looked serious, full of compassion and tenderness
and that touch of anxiety that always got to him. Earth
mother Darcie. He kept his hands off her with extreme
difficulty.

'You left without dancing with me,' she pouted like a
spoilt child. Patrick eyed her askance and she laughed
and flipped at her skirt as she wafted past him into the
house. She wandered around, looking at the completed
renovations, remarking upon them. The floorboards had
been sanded and polished, and thick beige rugs were
scattered around. The curving stair-rail and the
mezzanine balustrade were painted the despised
aubergine colour. It looked, she told him with an air of

surprise, absolutely right. She seemed a bit lost for a few seconds then, but whirled over to the stereo and flipped through his records.

'What we need is dance music. Dankworth and Laine—that'll do just fine.' She put the record on and, smiling brilliantly, whirled around as Cleo Laine's smoky voice began.

Patrick's eyes narrowed. 'You're drunk,' he said.

'Drunk? On two glasses of champagne and a crate of self-respect?' Laughing, she swayed to the music, holding her arms out to him. The stuff of dreams, Patrick thought.

'More like a crate of champagne. I hope you came by cab.' He sidestepped her affectionate embrace and headed for the kitchen. That generous affection of hers got to him too. In more ways than one. 'I'll make some coffee. You'd better drink it black.'

She tore after him, and stood fuming while he filled the percolator and switched it on. Amused, he wondered which would come to the boil first.

'I don't want your damned coffee! Damn you, Patrick—how dare you just slip away from the party like that when you *knew* it was you I wanted more than anyone else, because I—well, because you are the only one who knows just how much that race meant to me?' She stepped back and glared at him. 'You didn't even drink a glass of champagne in my honour!'

'That's because I'm flying tomorrow.'

'*One* glass wouldn't have hurt,' she scowled, watching him set out some cups. 'Is it another business trip?'

Another look at a some tanneries in the state's north-west and a call in Brisbane, he told her. 'I'll be away two days. Why don't you sit down?'

She didn't sit down. Patrick folded his arms and leaned back against the counter to watch her drift around the kitchen, absently touching things like a child trying to get up the nerve to confess something. She turned her head quickly and met his eyes, and he received another kick to the vitals.

'You could have danced with me,' she said. '*Dancing* before a flight is surely not considered a hazard.'

He laughed wryly. 'It depends. I wasn't in the mood.'

'Not in the *mood*! What happened? At the track you were so—I mean, I thought you were *with* me, I thought you *understood*. I wanted to celebrate with you, Patrick. I wanted to *talk* to you about it and share this terrific feeling of being alive again, and what do I get from you? Black coffee! Stupid me, I thought you had some sensitivity, but you're about as sensitive as a—a centurion tank!'

That got to him. 'Lady, you don't know just how sensitive I'm being.' He grasped her wrist as she headed for the door, swung her around to face him, cursing as he saw the glitter of tears in her eyes. That got to him, too. Let's face it, everything about Darcie got to him. Sighing, he pulled her close. 'You were superb today. Magnificent. I was watching through glasses when you went into that spin.' Patrick closed his eyes momentarily, remembering the drenching fear like nothing he'd ever experienced. 'I thought I understood about your nightmares, and I thought I knew the kind of fear you felt for Matt, but when you spun around right in the path of the other cars . . . it gave me some idea of what it took for you to go out there again.'

'You don't know how *good* it feels, Patrick! It was—it was *fantastic*!' She pulled away from him and pirouetted around the kitchen. He laughed at her exuberance. Her dress was as blue as her eyes and the skirt flared out, giving glimpses of her glorious legs. 'No one else *knows,* and I was so tired of being consoled for losing when I'd *won,* and that's why I had to see you. You are the only person I can celebrate with.' Her eyes sparkled, she threw back her head and laughed, hugging herself. Then she came over and hugged him, and hitched up on her toes to look in his eyes. 'Thank you, Patrick,' she said, and kissed him jubilantly on the mouth. Sweet heaven, he thought, standing stock still. Drawing back, she stared at him, her mouth parted, her breath excited and uneven. Eyes half-closed, she leaned close and pressed her mouth against his, keeping it there chastely like a girl trying a first kiss. It was a little tentative, gauche even, but it rocked him. She drew the tip of her tongue along his lower lip and delicately inside as his mouth opened.

Abruptly, he grasped her arms, holding her strongly away from him. 'Darcie—are you seducing me?'

'Yes,' she smiled. 'What are you going to do about it?'

'You're high as a kite. I'll take you home before you do something you might regret. Did anyone know you were coming here?'

Her eyes danced. 'You're not worrying about what people might think, Patrick, darling?'

'*You* might be worried tomorrow.'

' "We're both of age and unattached," ' she quoted him, unfastening the top button of his shirt. 'And you're not even my boss any more—it's hardly scandalous, is it? This is a very tasteful shirt,' she said, stroking the fabric over his chest. 'I'm glad you let me reform your lousy taste in clothes.'

He caught her hands and stilled them, but she laughed and swayed deliberately against him, making him suck in his breath sharply.

'Of course,' she said, casting him a look that would melt steel, 'you might not want me.'

Patrick held her grimly away from him. 'I wanted you the first time you kissed me on that roundabout,' he said harshly. 'And I've wanted you ever since, as you know very well.'

He looked down at her flushed, sparkling face. All the intriguing, maddening things that made her what she was were there to be seen. The hint of primness behind the passion, the promise of temper behind the deep, generous compassion, that faint mist of anxiety behind the renewed, blazing confidence. She was a bottomless, emotional well. Yet, when she wanted, she had the cold precision of a competitive racer. A man might spend the rest of his life finding the extent of Darcie. 'I should take you home.' He groaned inwardly, hearing the lack of resolution in his voice. Involuntarily, his hands loosened on her and she was close again, filling his arms, fragrant and soft and willing. Her hair was silky against his cheek and he turned his face into it. He knew his place in her life, dammit. As she said, she'd needed him while she found herself again. And as soon as she began to succeed, he'd lost her little by little to her old life. There was a certain irony in that, Patrick thought. She had made it now, and she was here for all the wrong reasons, and he should tell her so. He moved her back so that he could look at her while he delivered another brutal truth she wouldn't like, but she smiled at him and he bent and kissed her instead. And she moved against him and the contours of her beautiful body flowed beneath his palms and fingertips, and it was a heroic effort to offer her one last chance of retreat.

'You're going to hate me in the morning,' he said harshly.

'No, I'm not,' she whispered, sliding her arms around him. 'I'm going to love you in the morning.'

Love you, the words echoed in his head. She's drunk, he reminded himself. High on champagne and self-esteem. 'You don't know what you're saying,' he said thickly, lifting her into his arms. 'And, heaven help me, I don't care.'

He took her to bed. And he astonished her. Already Darcie knew that there were depths to Patrick that weren't on public show, already she knew that he had the capacity to surprise her, but still he astonished her. His passion and power were matched by his tenderness, his crushing strength by the delicacy of his touch. One minute he had her surrounded, overwhelmed by his sheer muscle power, and the next she would be sighing, arching at the touch of a single fingertip.

A dozen times she almost said 'I love you', but showed him instead, loving him with tenderness and passion, with her undisguised responses to his touch, with her eager attention to his needs. He loved her, too, she knew it. She had been loved before and she knew how it was to be loved. It was in the way he held her and cared to please her, and he didn't have to say 'I love you'. The words were a technicality.

'You are such a beautiful man,' she said once, as she ran her hands down over the rough and the smooth of him. He snorted at the adjective, and rolled over with her beneath him, so that all the long, broad, rough and smooth length of him was impressed upon her.

'The beauty is all yours,' he murmured, and raised himself on one elbow to curve a hand to her breast. He looked at it as if it were a work of art in a gallery. Darcie found it extraordinarily arousing. 'That day in the park,' she said a little breathlessly as he stroked his thumb back and forth, 'when you retrieved the keys . . . did you . . . er . . .?'

Slowly, provocatively, he smiled. 'Straight in and straight out. Cross my heart.' But it was her heart he crossed. 'Not to say I wasn't tempted to look.' His fingertips stroked the swell of her breasts, repeating the motions that drew the longest sighs from her. 'But I decided if I *did* touch, I wanted you conscious and looking just the way you are now.'

A faint ripple of unease passed over her at that, but it was lost as Patrick fondled her, finding new ways to take her breath away. He slid down in the bed and put his mouth to her breasts, and she cried out as the pleasure pierced her, took her half-way to fulfilment.

'Not yet,' he told her, eyes glittering in the honey light of the lamp, and he moved a little further away, holding her, kissing her pale skin as he went, and, the further away he went, the closer he was, which seemed to Darcie only proper for a man of such ambiguity. 'Not yet,' he said again as she called his name, but later the moment came.

'Darcie?' he asked huskily, as if there could possibly be a question to be answered when she was wrapped around him, waiting for him.

'Yes,' she urged, keeping her eyes on his, gasping her wonderment as he filled her, seeing his pleasure, letting him see hers. In mutual amazement they stared into each other's eyes, smiling in a moment of stillness before the slow fuse they'd set reached its limit. And the night went up in smoke and Darcie cried out, and hardly heard her own voice as a train went down the line a few streets away, blasting its horn, filling the room, shaking it with the roar and the rhythm of its passing.

Later, Darcie sat propped in Patrick's arms, her head tilted in to his shoulder. She smiled. Yawned.

'I love the sound of trains,' she said dreamily. 'I love you, Patrick.'

CHAPTER NINE

IT WAS dawn when Darcie woke. She stretched, she yawned. She looked at the intricate beamed ceiling, the wrong-coloured walls. Then she sat up quickly and looked at the empty pillow beside her. Smiling, she trailed a hand across it. Patrick must be in the bathroom. She got up and went to the window, raising the blind to lean on the sill and gaze down into his courtyard. There were the rose-bushes she'd chosen for him, and three more tubs full of soil, but unplanted as yet. Darcie's smile dimmed. A vague uneasiness intruded on her contentment. Something she couldn't pin down. She didn't hear him come in. His arms came around her from behind and pulled her back against him. She wasn't wearing anything, as her nervous system swiftly reminded her. 'Morning,' he murmured against her neck.

'Hello,' she said idiotically, feeling his close inspection.

'You're blushing,' he said.

'Of course not. What are you going to plant in the tubs?'

He chuckled at her evasion, and she felt every little vibration along her spine. He wasn't wearing anything, either.

'More roses, I think. If you'll give me some more advice.'

She turned in his arms and her nerves screamed with

delight.

'Now?' she asked, eyes wide and smiling as she clasped her arms around his neck.

'We could talk about it, I suppose,' he murmured, inching her back towards the bed. She gave a little scream as he hooked a foot around her ankle and toppled backwards on to the bed, with her sprawled inelegantly on top of him.

'I want some of those big pink blowsy ones,' he told her.

'They sound positively indecent,' she giggled.

'There's no such thing as an indecent rose.' He studied her, his eyes full of warmth and amusement. 'You're blushing again. Thinking about last night?'

'No. I'm thinking about this morning.'

'Good. This morning will be beautiful.'

'Last night was beautiful.'

'This morning will be better.'

'Impossible.'

'I never can resist a challenge,' he growled, and, watching her fiercely through half-closed eyes, he lifted her over him, held her there for a moment to anticipate the delights of the morning, then, smiling at her gradually widening eyes, let her appreciate bit by bit all it had to offer.

The dawn light strengthened and threw a soft rose-glow over the tangled bedclothes. Patrick sat against the pillows and Darcie leaned on him, contented. 'I thought you were crazy to buy a place near a railway line,' she murmured, 'but I think I like the sound of trains.'

'So you said last night,' he said, and his laughter was a minor earthquake behind her.

'What's so funny?' she asked, turning her head.

'I've got to know the timetables. There was no train last night.'

'Of course there was! Last night when we—er—while we were—er—a goods train, I think. It was going very fast and seemed to go on forever. There was another one this morning, just a little while ago when we were—er——' She stopped, her eyes widening. 'Oh!'

'A fast goods train that went on forever! Did you see stars too, darling?' he mocked and, laughing, ducked the pillow she threw at him.

He pulled her back against him and stroked her hair, and she thought he was about to say something more, but a silence fell. There was no hurry, she thought, for all the things they would say to each other. But one thing she wanted him to know now was that he was the only man in her life since Gavin. In his mind, she knew, was the suspicion that she'd succumbed to Fitz, a suspicion she hadn't exactly discouraged, and she didn't want him to think that. But she was reluctant to mention another man's name at a perfect moment like this. Instead, she smiled out at the hazy sunrise and said, 'You were right. Three years is a long time.' He didn't answer, but she felt his sudden slight tension and knew he had understood what she was saying. She waited a while, a little disappointed that he said nothing in return.

And a cool breeze floated in from somewhere as that faint uneasiness returned. This time she pinned it down. Patrick hadn't said he loved her. And he had her declaration. Darcie reminded herself that she was a mature woman and not a lovestruck, mooning teenager who thought words more important than deeds. She knew how it felt to be loved and she was feeling it.

Turning to smile at him, she said, 'Would you really sue me if I drove with Fitz?'

'Yes. But I wouldn't enjoy it.'

'That makes all the difference.' She grimaced. 'Are you sure you didn't come on a bit heavy about that because you were jealous?'

'No,' he said and met her eyes blandly. 'No, I'm not sure. But I wouldn't advise you to call my bluff by driving with Fitzgibbon.'

'You're a hard man,' she said, nettled even though it didn't matter any more. 'As it happens, I don't intend to race again at all.'

He turned her around, studied her closely. 'You're retiring?'

'I had to finish it off properly by racing again, I suppose. But now—I'm going to bring my trophies out of hiding and polish them up and put them where they ought to be.'

'You're sure it's what you want?'

'I don't have what it takes any more. I'm beginning to wonder if I ever did.'

He snorted. 'Thousands would disagree.'

'There's a psychologist called Johnsgard in America who did a study on racing drivers. He said they have very low guilt levels, less need to accept blame or punish themselves than other people, and little or no nurturing instincts. When I was younger I think I fitted the description, but—maybe because I'm female—I've changed. Women reach an age when they want to be needed, to nurture . . .' Darcie hesitated. Considering the circumstances, it was another declaration, and she waited for a few moments, half hoping he would pick up his cue. He said nothing and she rushed on, embarrassed and vaguely apprehensive. 'Anyway, bringing up Matt seems to have brought out a side of me that is at odds with the race game. I couldn't be single-minded enough any more. I couldn't be detached enough. So,' she finished briskly, 'yesterday was my last race.'

'What will you do?' he asked.

The morning was losing its glow. Was she naïve to have thought they might now be talking about 'us' instead of 'you'? Had she misread all those signals he'd given her? Surely not, when she was still radiant, body and soul, from his loving. 'I haven't decided,' she said lightly. 'One of the car mags is making noises about me writing a column for them aimed at women consumers, I've had an approach about making some training-films for road safety, one to work for a prestige car company.' Darcie slid out of bed and threw him a brilliant smile to hide her sudden monumental uncertainty. 'Mind if I use the shower first?'

Darcie used the shower, put on her blue dress, and wandered through Patrick's house while he showered. The renovations were finished and effective. More than that. They were lovely. Quiet and masculine without severity. She frowned, as she viewed the mezzanine sitting-room which was a mellow mix of neutrals and greens. Very tasteful. And Patrick had chosen all these colours himself? How could a man who wore brazen Paisley ties, years out of date, choose a colour scheme with such subtlety? Even the spare bedroom was attractive and homey.

Darcie went in to look at the suburban view from the window and nearly fell over a suitcase. She leaned across and opened the blind, and saw that there were other suitcases, and full too, as she discovered when she tried to push them out of her way. 'Chicago', 'Munich', 'Sydney' appeared in various pairings on a profusion of labels around the handles. There were thick black pen lines crossed over some of them, and words scrawled. Munich. Now who had mentioned Munich lately? Darcie squeezed past and looked at the view, but something about the suitcases bothered her. Her eyes kept going back to them and, when she noticed that the fastenings on one were open, she knelt and lifted the lid.

It was packed with men's clothes, all neatly folded, but disturbed as if items had been withdrawn. On top was a formal tucked white shirt with black stud buttons. At first she thought it was the one she'd chosen with Patrick, but it bore a different label. Beneath it was a black dinner jacket. Under that a mid-grey suit very similar to the one he'd recently bought at her urging. Shirts, also impeccable, in pale blue and neat stripes, rolls of silk ties in subtle colours. All quality, all expensive. All tasteful. She held up the dinner jacket and frowned at it. Patrick's size. Everything was in Patrick's size. Bending, she studied the suitcase labels again, and by the time he came to the door she understood.

She stood up, the formal shirt draped over her arm. Patrick looked at it and the open suitcase and said drily, 'Oh.'

'My goodness, I was given enough hints, wasn't I?' she snapped, her eyes kindling. 'You hinted at the outset that there might be a perfectly good explanation for your lousy clothes. You almost slipped up and told me when I was here once that you were wearing all your old stuff that had been in storage while you were overseas. And Mark said something about your proper clothes turning up in Munich, and you made out that he was rambling because of the anaesthetic!'

Patrick looked a bit sheepish. He leaned against the door-frame, his hair damp from the shower, his chest bare and a towel draped around his hips. 'When I came back home, some of my luggage was lost. All my suits and shirts, sports gear—everything, really.'

'Except for your shoes,' she said tartly, 'and your jeans and your monogrammed handkerchiefs. You took up rowing and put on all that muscle—"a whole shirt size in six months"—and that's why your lousy old shirts and jackets didn't fit properly!'

'When I bought that stuff I didn't have much money,' he explained.

'And no taste!'

'I admit it.'

'You must have a mean streak. You should have bought some new stuff as soon as you got here.'

He shrugged. 'I just didn't have the time—and I told you, clothes aren't of major importance to me. Mine had gone missing, but my old gear was here, so I used it, thinking my luggage would turn up any day.'

'And they *did* turn up, but you asked me to go shopping for clothes with you anyway, and let me talk you into buying things *exactly* like those you already had!' She remembered his meek behaviour and his secret amusement, remembered his wistful fingerings of flashy ties and the black and white striped dinner-shirt with frills and Liberace buttons, and she felt like a prize idiot.

He grinned. 'I thought you'd see through it, honestly. And I was going to tell you.'

'Tell me what? That you actually have perfect taste in clothes, just as you apparently have in home decorating? That you didn't need my help at all, but just enjoyed making a damned fool out of me? I suppose you're an expert on roses, too—did it give you a few laughs seeing me take your damned rose-bushes so seriously?'

'It wasn't like that—it started as a joke when you fussed over me, brushing me down, and I kind of liked it, so I just——'

'Let me think you were a great helpless ape with no taste!' she fumed. 'I hope you were entertained whenever I clucked over your ties and those awful suits——'

'No, honestly,' he said, but his mouth twitched and she saw red.

'You pig, Patrick!' she yelled, and shot past him, flinging the shirt in his face. 'How dare you amuse yourself at my expense? I wish I'd let you buy that flashy brown suit. You would have had to wear it, and you would have looked like a—a—dodgy used-car salesman, and it would have served you right!'

She ran back to his bedroom, averting her eyes from the rumpled bed, and grabbed her shoes. When he caught her arm she whirled away into the hall and down the stairs.

'Darcie—wait—this is ridiculous, unimportant.'

In the lounge she snatched her bag from the table where she'd left it in a euphoric haze to make love to him, so sure had she been that he loved her. But he didn't love her. Darcie knew now why she'd been so uneasy. Patrick was not the strong, silent type. Patrick said what he thought, said what he felt, as she'd discovered to her cost in the past. If he loved her he would say without frills, 'I love you.' The truth, the whole truth, and nothing but the truth—ninety-nine per cent of the time. One per cent of the time he said nothing. He was a decent, tender lover, and decent, tender lovers didn't say, 'I *don't* love you.' 'No comment at all is occasionally kinder than the truth,' he'd told her. She'd told him she loved him, and he'd made no comment.

Furiously, she scrubbed tears from her eyes. He didn't love her, and he didn't need her, either. Not even to help him with his rotten clothes. She felt so stupid, so idiotic, but that hurt her so much. It was her odd, maternal feelings prompted by his awful suits and shirts and ties that had got her involved with him, and it was all a sham! A great big joke that had blown up in her face like a firecracker. 'Damn you, Patrick!' she spat as he caught up with her. He grabbed her wrist and, after a short tussle, reeled her in. His skin was damp and the towel was wet and he smelled wonderful. A knife turned in Darcie's chest.

'Let me go. I—I wish I hadn't come here last night!'

He stiffened. 'I did point out that you might have regrets in the morning.'

'Well, I *do*!' she flared, hurting inside. She'd been so *sure*, so arrogantly, humiliatingly sure. 'I was a challenge to you, I suppose, Patrick. You don't enjoy things that come too easy—you bulldozed your way into Ensigns and relished the fight to change the old guard. You probably would have forgotten all about sponsoring Matt if I hadn't put obstacles in your way! And if I'd said yes that first time and gone to dinner with you, I dare say you wouldn't have bothered with me again. But you never could resist the door marked "No Entry", you always had to trespass beyond the "No Trespassers" sign. You always had to play in the playground that was out of bounds!'

'For a man with a mission, I passed up several opportunities,' he pointed out. 'With very little persuasion I could have had you here one night. You do remember that?'

She flushed at the crude reminder. 'It was much more effective to back off and give me space. You waited, and you worked on me so cleverly, letting me think you were hopeless at choosing clothes because you knew that got to me, because I like to feel needed. Damn you!' she yelled over him as he said something in protest. 'In the end I came to *you*. In the end it was *me* persuading *you*. Well, how do you think I feel to know I was just a challenge to you?'

'And what was I to you?' he growled. 'A handy male to take to bed when you'd finally rediscovered your libido? What happened, did Fitzgibbon pass out from too much drink?'

She sucked in her breath sharply and lashed out at him, and this time he wasn't quick enough to block it. Her hand slapped square on his jaw with enough force to whip his head to one side.

Horrified, Darcie fled to the front door, but he was too fast for her. He caught her, and swung her around into his arms.

'Darcie—forget I said that,' he said, with a look of self-disgust. 'Why don't we sit down and talk this out?'

'What is there to talk about?'

He hesitated a moment. 'The future. What we're going to do.'

Darcie's heart gave a great thump. 'Do?'

'Last night,' he said slowly, 'you didn't know what you were doing, but this morning . . .' He stopped, and she thought for a moment that he seemed unsure of himself. A very odd notion to have about Patrick, and one soon dispelled as he gave her one of those academic looks that she hated and went on briskly, 'What I'm saying is, whatever we have between us is worth following up.'

Her back stiffened. 'Oh, it is, is it?'

'Our timing was lousy and our motives all wrong, but you have to admit, we proved that we're compatible.' This last was said with unmistakable confidence, verging on smugness. He stood there, naked to the waist, sticking out his chest as if to say, 'You know you can't live without this.' And he was probably right, damn him.

'And what are your conclusions, Patrick?' she enquired, her eyes beginning to sparkle dangerously.

'Why don't you move in with me?'

'All the romance of a wet sandbag,' she flung at him. 'You stand there talking about "compatibility" and "following-up" on our lovemaking, as if it's one of your damned company reports! Compatibility! Last night I said I loved you!'

'Last night you loved everybody,' he said drily. 'Don't worry, I won't hold you to that if you move in with me.'

Darcie stepped back a pace. She loved him, but he wouldn't hold her to it. And she wanted to be held to it. Desolation filled her. Only pride stopped her howling.

'No thanks, Patrick. You were right the first time. I didn't know what I was doing!'

'Don't——' he began to say, and made a grab for her wrist as she opened the door. 'Don't . . .' But he appeared to run out of words again. He pulled her roughly into his arms and kissed her with a clumsy fierceness that was unlike him, for the first time using his great physical strength to hold her. It startled more than frightened her, but he released her abruptly when she made sounds of protest in her throat. Her hand, clutching at his shoulder, fell away from him, brushing down his bare, broad centurion chest. Turning away quickly, she flung open the door on the beautiful morning. He'd promised her a beautiful morning, she remembered. Outside, she flung him one last glowering look.

'There's one good thing to come out of all this—you can burn those lousy Paisley ties now!'

It was still early morning when she arrived home. Matt was eating breakfast in the kitchen and she was deeply embarrassed. As a role model, she was an abject failure.

'And what time do you call this?' he nagged, mimicking her voice. 'This is unforgivable! You're grounded for a week, kid!'

She laughed, bit her lip. 'I'm sorry. Were you worried?'

'Worried?' Matt screeched in a falsetto, then grinned and went on normally, 'Nope. Partied on and didn't miss you for ages. And Mark said you were with Rick.'

She looked up sharply, her colour rising again. 'How did he know that?'

He shrugged, suddenly a little awkward. 'Dad wouldn't mind, you know, Darcie. He wouldn't want you to be alone.'

'And what about you, Matt?'

'Er—give me time,' he said honestly. Darcie smiled. He might be impatient to fly the nest, but he didn't necessarily want the nest to change. Matt looked at her across the table and she saw that he was really seeing her, the woman, and not just the familiar mother-image he'd taken for granted. She'd reluctantly let go of the schoolboy, and he was reluctantly letting go of her. All part of the pattern. 'You'll have all the time you want,' she said drily. 'Things aren't what they seem.'

What was she going to do now, she thought gloomily as she changed into her overalls at Harry's garage. Cut all but business ties with Patrick? There was no going back to being good friends. Becoming lovers had made that impossible. She felt a terrible grief for the loss of that friendship—and all for nothing, for she couldn't accept what Patrick offered in its place. She was not psychologically equipped for a no-strings affair with him. There were certain prerequisites for a carefree mistress, just as there were for a successful racing driver, and she didn't have them. Mistress, driver, mother—she was running out of roles, Darcie thought in dark humour. She wondered if Patrick had thrown out his horrible Paisley ties yet. Maybe she should have asked for one as a souvenir.

Late September. Darcie accepted the offer of a ladies' column in the car magazine. They called it *Girls' Torque*. She went into training on a word-processor and typed copy at night, mending cars by day. Matt divided his time between study, cars and photo sessions for the Ensigns campaign. Darcie was invited to do a commentary segment at the Adelaide Grand Prix in November. Kev's leg came out of plaster, photos of a thriving Stephen James proliferated on her notice-board, Darcie's roses were blooming, the canary next door sang, the sun shone. Darcie polished her trophies and displayed them in a beautiful new cabinet. It was ironic, she often thought as she looked on them with pleasure, that now that she had the past in its proper place, the future was giving her trouble.

Patrick no longer called at the house. Darcie's only information about him came via Matt and Mark, both of whom were mystified by the sudden rise and fall in their relationship. Patrick, they told her, was away more and more often as he finalised the purchase of the tannery and looked around for other related country properties for Ensigns. She always casually checked to discover if he'd flown safely back after each trip. Dismally, she wondered if she would always need to do so. She pictured herself, grey-haired and wrinkled, phoning around to see if Patrick was safely on the ground. But Patrick was the indestructible type, and she never truly expected to hear that he hadn't returned. So one morning, when Mark phoned her at the garage to tell her that Patrick's plane was overdue, she thought she had a bad connection.

'I thought you'd want to know, my dear,' Mark said.

The stark news rocked her. She sat down abruptly. 'How late is he?'

'Two hours. In his last radio contact he said he had engine trouble and was losing height over mountainous country near the border. Rain-forest country,' Mark added reluctantly. 'But he gave them a position, so . . .'

She remembered flying over rain forest with Patrick. Remembered thinking that anything could be on the ground beneath the thick green canopy and remain unseen. Oh, no, she thought, fighting the images that came. Not Patrick.

'A reconnaissance plane is out looking for him.'

'He's a good pilot,' she croaked. 'It could be something quite minor. He might not have crashed. He'll be all right.'

'Of course he will,' Mark said, too heartily. 'I've phoned Barbara and Maurice—his parents—we'll just have to wait.'

She phoned Matt with the news, and forced herself back to work. But the images blinded her—Patrick unconscious and bleeding in the crashed plane, Patrick thrown out on impact and maimed, Patrick against a familiar, nightmare background of flames and smoke. An hour later she downed tools and told Harry what had happened. 'Gee, I'm sorry,' Harry said, 'I like the big fella. Of course you can have the afternoon off.'

Darcie went to the aerodrome, with the illogical feeling that, if there was someone waiting there for him, Patrick was more likely to return. She found comfort in the sight and the droning sound of other small planes flying in. Sooner or later, one of them would be Patrick's, she told herself.

Four hours overdue. Control relayed the information that the reconnaissance plane had found nothing, but that visibility had been hampered when rain and heavy mist had swept in over the mountainous area. If it worsened, it would delay any full-scale search.

Darcie drank some coffee from a drinks machine. She phoned Sara and talked to her sister-in-law and listened to the gurgles of her godson until she ran out of coins for the phone. She wished she could talk to her parents, but they were somewhere on the road between Mackay and Brisbane. Darcie felt the fear build up inside her, and with it the chill loneliness that might, she realised, become permanent if Patrick didn't come back.

Matt came a little later. His handsome young face was manfully stoic, but as she took his hand for comfort she knew she was giving back as much as she received.

One by one, others came to wait for Patrick.

Mark, in his elegant Italian suit.

A little, worried woman who sat by herself for a time before she came over and said she recognised Darcie from her picture in the newspaper. 'Mr Stafford's got it pinned up in his study,' she said, then confided that she was Hazel Simmons, his housekeeper, and she'd just finished 'doing' his place out when her cousin, who worked at Ensigns—and who'd put her on to the housekeeper's job, by the way, and eternally grateful she was, too—phoned to tell her that Mr Stafford was missing. 'I was on my way home and thought I'd pop in and see if there was any news. Well,' she said, looking around at them as if they had demanded a legitimate reason for her concern, 'he's a lovely man, isn't he?'

And eventually, Patrick's parents came. Barbara Stafford, cool and controlled in an ice-blue suit with silk shirt, kid gloves, pearls, with a mink-trimmed coat slung around her shoulders. She laid her cheek briefly against Mark's. Maurice Stafford, tall and slim, his good living beginning to show around his waist, shrewd grey eyes, hair silvering at the temples, handshake firm as he greeted Mark. They were introduced to everyone else. Barbara Stafford didn't recognise Darcie, who had driven her several times in the company Rolls. She bestowed an absent lady-of-the-manor smile upon them all. It only wavered when Hazel Simmons revealed herself as her son's housekeeper, grasped both Barbara's gloved hands and told her everything was going to be all right, because God wouldn't be so cruel as to take such a lovely man so young.

Darcie watched Patrick's parents curiously. They showed no outward signs of distress. Yet they had flown from Melbourne to wait for news of their son.

Time passed. It took the fear of loss to put things clearly into perspective, Darcie thought. Patrick cared for her, he liked her, he was a friend, a confidant, a tender, unselfish, exciting lover. When she was with him, she *felt* loved. A man could offer a declaration of love, yet offer less than Patrick. That he might be unable to offer it forever seemed suddenly less important in the face of never. She felt a twinge of regret as she relinquished her dream of a secure, permanent future lavish with children. If Patrick came back she would take what he offered and gamble on it lasting. If he came back. She closed her eyes and said out loud, firmly, 'When.'

'Pardon?' Mark said.

'*When* he comes back,' she said fiercely. 'Not *if*.' And Patrick's mother looked more closely at her then, more critically, more thoughtfully, as mothers do when another woman cares about a son.

The search was being delayed until the low cloud-cover shifted. Another hour at least, they were told. Barbara Stafford removed her gloves and, grimacing, accepted a cup of coffee from the machine. She spilled a little on her ice-blue suit. Maurice Stafford smoked several cigarettes. His hand trembled slightly, Darcie noticed. Their distress was there, but not for public display.

'He always was a tearaway,' Maurice said suddenly. 'Remember that time when he borrowed another boy's bike and went riding all around the streets for

hours and hours. We were frantic. Thought he'd been
kidnapped or fallen under a bus . . . he was about
seven, I think——'

Six, Darcie corrected mentally.

'He was six,' his mother said out loud.

'We phoned the hospitals and we had the police
there when he came back. He'd been gone for four
hours, and he strolled in calm as you please and asked
the policeman if he would take him for a ride in the
police car with the siren on.' He laughed, squinting
his eyes into his cigarette smoke. 'When we asked him
why he'd borrowed the bike, he said he'd seen a park
from his bedroom window—it was when we had the
penthouse, you remember, Mark? Twenty-first
floor—and he'd been trying to find this park because
he wanted to ride on a special swing or something——'

'Roundabout,' Darcie said absently. 'He wanted to
ride on the roundabout.'

Both Maurice and Barbara turned to her this time,
appraising this woman to whom their son had told
childhood stories. Their quick glance at each other
reminded her that she had come directly from the
garage and, although she had stripped off her greasy
overalls, was wearing jeans and a sweater and the
scuffed sneakers she used for work. Her hair was
pulled into a practical pony-tail, and her hasty
cleaning had left a fine rim of black beneath her nails.
Looking at her hands, Barbara Stafford said politely,
'Mark didn't say what you did.'

'I'm a mechanic,' Darcie said, and Mark informed
his sister that this was the Darcie Miller he'd often
talked about, the racing driver. But Barbara Stafford
couldn't take her eyes off Darcie's fingernails. There

was a certain humour in the situation that Patrick would enjoy, Darcie thought. She got up and went to the window to scan the sky that stubbornly matched Patrick's prosaic description. It was the colour of old, faded jeans.

CHAPTER TEN

JUST as Darcie and Patrick had talked of Mark when he lay in danger on the operating-table, so now they talked more and more of Patrick, keeping him real and alive.

He is a very good pilot, his mother said, rather consciously using the present tense. Patrick is just naturally good at everything. Oh, in his early years he didn't concentrate at school, so he turned in very average results, but that was only because his mind was too quick and enquiring for the restriction of a classroom. Later, he excelled. He was good at sports from the time he could walk, Maurice reminisced; his drawing was way beyond his years; he was quick at maths; he was musical.

'Can he sing?' Darcie asked.

'Er . . .' Maurice Stafford fixed her with a look so like one of Patrick's that she blushed.

'It doesn't matter,' she said.

'We had to remind ourselves to give poor Michael centre stage now and then. In any other family he would have been a star, but he always struggled in Patrick's shadow.'

Maybe that was why poor Michael was always the one brought out to show off for visitors, Darcie thought. That, and Patrick's own disinclination to put on a show for anyone.

Patrick was a survivor, his father said firmly. Remember when he dived off an Olympic diving board when he was only eight? Came up grinning, not a nerve in his body. Remember the time he got on that horse, climbed that cliff, swam that river?

'I always lived in fear that something would happen to him,' Barbara confessed. She brushed away another coffee-spill from another cup of coffee. 'When they told me my son had drowned, I was so sure it was Patrick. Do you remember, Maurie?' she asked her husband, and her voice trembled. 'I kept saying it couldn't be Michael, that they'd made a mistake and it must be Patrick. He was always the one in trouble. To this day I don't know how it came to be Michael instead of Patrick who died.' Her control deserted her suddenly, and her breath sucked in on a high, distressing note. Blindly she turned to her husband and sobbed and gasped in his arms. 'No, no. Not Patrick too,' she cried out in anguish. Everyone averted their eyes. Matt got up, muttering something about finding out if there was any news. The loss of Barbara Stafford's monumental control was too awful to watch.

It was the same story, but with a sad twist, Darcie thought. They loved him. Ironically, it was probably Patrick who had been their favourite, not Michael. Maybe, fearing because of his fearlessness, they had been harder on him than on his twin. And after losing one son they might have been stricter still to preserve the other. Strict, busy parents, not given to shows of affection. A boy of eight, trying to come to terms with the death of his brother, mixing up his facts and his feelings could easily misinterpret that. Come home, Patrick, so that you'll know you got that old story wrong. Darcie concentrated on the thought for a long time. Come home, Patrick.

Her mind was wandering in a rain-forest jungle as Matt came back. He grinned, he laughed out loud. He broke into a gallop, leapt into the air and let out a yell that brought Darcie to her feet. 'He's OK! Patrick's OK!' He grabbed Darcie and whirled her around a couple of times. 'He went down in a clearing just before the cloud closed in. Lost a wing and rammed into some trees, knocked out the radio.' Matt related the details with boyish relish. 'He got some bumps and a few scratches when the glass shattered—one tree branch shoved through the screen and missed his head by *this* much.' He pinched his thumb and forefinger together, cheerfully dramatising his second-hand news. 'He knew the chances of being spotted weren't good, so he tried to light a fire, and the wet wood made plenty of smoke, but there was so much mist drifting about he figured no one would notice it. Then, you know what he did? He climbed up and hacked off bits of trees with the axe from the plane's emergency kit—so that they wouldn't totally obscure the plane——' he laughed, his eyes shining with admiration '—and he stuck sheets of paper all around.'

'Paper?' Mark said.

'Reports and things. You know he always carries stacks of files with him? Well, he speared computer print-outs in the trees like streamers, climbed up on the plane and plastered paper all over it. Everything was so damp, it stuck. The pilot who spotted him said he might never have gone in for a closer look but for the splashes of white. They're taking him out by chopper now.'

They shared their relief as they'd shared their fears. Darcie howled unashamedly and mopped up with a handkerchief she found in her jeans pocket. It was one of Patrick's, and she cried tears of thanks for his deliverance all over it. There was nothing more equalising than the fear of death, and even Barbara Stafford embraced everyone to celebrate the reprieve. The mood didn't last, of course. Later Darcie thought that Patrick's mother even resented them, for having seen her break down. That evening, when they met again at Sydney airport where Patrick was being flown in, it was as if those hours of agony hadn't happened. Barbara had changed from the ice-blue suit with its revealing coffee-stains, Maurice smoked cigarettes with a steady hand.

Darcie would never forget Patrick's home-coming that day. There were several people around him as he walked from the plane. They appeared to be asking questions, and he to be tiredly answering them, when he saw there were people waiting for him. Only Hazel Simmons had gone home upon the announcement of his rescue. 'Say hello for me,' she adjured Darcie. 'He's a lovely man.'

The lovely man stopped and looked straight at Darcie, and she wanted to run to him then, right along that beam of warmth that came from him, but she held back because his mother was here, and a mother who had come close to the horror of losing her second boy surely had first claim. Anxiously, Darcie checked him out. There was a plaster on his left hand, scratches on his neck and face and a bruise on his forehead. He wore his leather flying jacket over crumpled, patently borrowed clothes, and he carried an Ensigns bag. Darcie had never seen a more marvellous sight.

Matt, less sensitive to the prior claims of parents, bounded over to welcome Patrick. 'What happened to your hand? Did it go through the windscreen?'

'I hurt it attending to some paperwork,' Patrick said,

dead-pan.

'It's true, then?' Mark exclaimed. 'You really stuck reports all over the plane?'

'Over part of it, anyway.' He smiled at his uncle. 'It was your Financial Five Year Strategy that saved me—the only good it was ever likely to do, I might add.'

Mark cast his eyes upwards. '*Dear* boy,' he said, 'how I've missed you!'

Patrick turned again, then, to Darcie, but looked beyond her and saw his parents. 'Mum—Dad—what are you doing here?'

Barbara Stafford, cool and collected, laid a hand on his arm and kissed him on the cheek. 'We were beginning to worry,' she said, as if he'd turned up late for a dinner party. By comparison, Maurice's vigorous handshake and slaps on the shoulder seemed ostentatious. Darcie couldn't help contrasting this with her own family's unashamed demonstrativeness. It was like watching a small, tragic game of pass the parcel, Darcie thought. Love was in the parcel and it passed from hand to hand, but no one ever took the wrappings off. Patrick looked oddly vulnerable.

'I forgot,' Mark said rather drily at her side. 'There *is* something Patrick isn't good at.'

They loved him, but he wasn't quite sure that they did, because they weren't good at telling and he wasn't good at believing. Darcie's eyes opened wide at this new view of Patrick. He wasn't good at believing, she already knew that. He hadn't believed her when she told him she loved him. He lifted his head and Darcie met his eyes. As he guarded his lopsided gaze and made his face carefully bland, she thought, too late, Patrick Stafford. Too late. I'm beginning to understand.

She should have trusted her instincts. With Patrick she'd felt loved, and she was one of the fortunate ones who knew how it felt to be loved. All her life she'd been loved, by parents and brothers, by Gavin, by Matt. Even Mark. Patrick, for all his ability and assurance, might not be sure when he was loved.

With that in mind, she reviewed the night of the race from Patrick's point of view. 'You're high as a kite', he'd said of her. In fact, he'd made much of the fact that she'd had too much champagne. Well, of course, to a less assured Patrick it must have looked as if she had turned up at his place, a little drunk and euphoric with success, eager to expend all her 'saved-up passion', as he'd once put it. She'd said 'I love you', but, in the circumstances, a man unsure of himself could be forgiven for thinking it merely an impulsive way of saying thank you. 'Last night you loved everybody', he'd said. 'And what was I to you? A handy male to take to bed when you'd finally rediscovered your libido?' There it had been, his fear honestly stated and, because he'd apologised immediately afterwards, she had dismissed it as temper. But of course she could have done nothing else. The flaw in all her logical reasoning had been her assumption that Patrick was as confident, as sure in matters of the heart, as he was in everything else. And he wasn't.

They all went out to the car park. Darcie couldn't think of anything to say in front of everyone else, and didn't quite have the nerve to take Patrick aside. After all, she might be wrong. It might all be wishful thinking on her part. So it was a rather formal 'goodnight' that she exchanged with him before she turned away to her car. It was parked a long way from Matt's bike and Mark's limousine, and she was suddenly terribly tired.

All the strain of the day caught up with her and she leaned against the door as she inserted the key. Heavy footsteps came quickly behind her, and she turned around to see Patrick, grim-faced, the shadows of strain around his eyes and mouth. He said nothing, but tugged her bag from her grasp and set it on the roof of the car with a purposeful air. She just stood there, gaping at him, and he slid his hands around her waist and quite abruptly pulled her against him.

'I promised myself this while I was trying to bring that plane down in a space the size of your rose garden,' he told her, 'while I was lighting fires and clambering around trees and doing any fool thing I could to make sure I was found.' His hold on her was fierce, as if he feared she might slip through his fingers, and he nuzzled in to her hair, breathing in deep. 'Mmm, Darcie. The smell of you, the feel of you! I promised myself to hold you just once more if I got out in one piece. You brought me home, Darcie,' he whispered harshly against her mouth. He kissed her with great hunger, with a rough eloquence, with the frankness that typified Patrick. Then she was free and he was gone. His footsteps thudded quickly away, there was the slam of a door and the smooth purr of Mark's car.

She slumped against her car and grinned like an idiot while tears poured down her face. She'd brought him home. Darling Patrick. He hadn't said he loved her, but he'd told her every time he'd touched her and a million times when he hadn't. And he'd told her again tonight. Eventually she got in the car and drove home and, halfway there, she got out at some traffic lights and sheepishly retrieved her shoulder-bag from the roof of the car.

Patrick was tied up with officialdom the following morning. 'Standard procedure following a forced landing,' Mark told her on the phone. 'Apparently they were able to establish that there was a fuel-line blockage, so it's pretty much a formality.'

'Does he seem OK today?'

'He has a clean bill of health from the doctor. Otherwise he's a bit grim, though fractionally better than last night, I have to admit. One minute he was in a foul mood, and then Barbara asked him something very ordinary and he burst out laughing. Delayed shock, I suppose.'

'What was it his mother said?'

'She asked him why on earth you would want to know if he could sing.'

Darcie gave a hiccup of laughter. So he *had* remembered that ridiculous conversation, had he? She pretended not to hear the query in Mark's voice.

'How long do you think he'll be tied up?'

'Until around one, I should say. I'm not sure where you'd find him after that.'

Darcie stared into space. 'I think I know where he'll be.'

She drove around a bit before she found the right hangar. Then she settled down to wait, remembering the first time she'd waited in the Rolls for him to fly in. That powerful feeling of welcome should have told her then what she knew now. A Cessna buzzed in across the blue to circle the field. She watched it descend, then touch down lightly like a droning, perky insect alighting on a tree branch. She watched it taxi around and align itself with the row of aircraft in front of the hangar.

There were a dozen signs on the rear of the hangar where she waited, forbidding entry to all but pilots and instructors and other authorised personnel. But Darcie saw Patrick silhouetted in the light at the other end and started down towards him. In the end she was running and Patrick saw her and so was he, and when they met he wrapped his arms around her and her feet left the ground as he kissed her. Darcie held him, thinking that that other time had, after all, been a pale forerunner of this. Patrick was here and holding her, and a missing part of herself had been restored.

He set her down and, breathlessly, they looked at each other.

'My mother seems to think you love me,' he said.

'Mothers know these things.'

'I didn't think mine would.'

'She cried, Patrick,' she said.

'She cried again last night.'

Pass the parcel, Darcie thought, and some of the wrappings had come off.

'I guessed you'd be flying today if you could. Making sure you didn't lose your nerve.' She grimaced. 'Smarter than waiting six years, like me.'

'If I waited six years, I doubt I'd *ever* find the nerve again, like you.' He touched her hair, her face, with that light, light touch that was so amazing. 'You remember meeting me in the Rolls here once? I came out and saw you, and damned near broke my neck getting to you. Couldn't believe how much I'd missed you. It set me back a bit. There I was, thinking I was more or less in control, and suddenly I was in a tail-spin.'

She smiled. 'I know all about spins. Very disorientating.'

He kissed her slowly, thoroughly, there in the hangar full of dismantled planes and grinning mechanics making jokes about scenes from *Casablanca*.

'*Very* disorientating,' she repeated breathlessly as they walked on. Patrick collected a bag and his suit jacket and they emerged into the sunshine. His car wasn't there, and neither was the Rolls. Patrick indicated her blue Toyota.

'Going my way?' he asked, grey eyes smiling.

'Yes, sir,' she said, unlocking the doors. 'I love you. Didn't you think I could be serious when I told you so that night?'

'You told me you loved trains, too,' he said drily.

'You thought I was drunk.'

'You did giggle a lot.'

'I was nervous. I wanted to tell you I loved you the moment you opened the door, but you looked at me like a stern headmaster.'

'It seemed to me that you wouldn't have been there at all except for the race and the champagne. Not the greatest boost to a man's ego.'

'Two glasses of champagne, that's all. I knew exactly what I was doing.'

'Yeah, well—it didn't look that way. It was always on the cards you'd go off like a firecracker one day, and there you were, fizzing and ready to explode, and I thought you'd chosen me to—to . . .'

'Explode with?'

He gave a grunt of laughter. 'Because you trusted me as much as anything else.'

'Loved you. I waited to see if I loved you before I threw myself at you. Why do you think I backed off so fast that other night at your place?'

'The night we painted the town aubergine,' he

murmured, a glint in his eye.

'I didn't love you then, but the chemistry was so good that I nearly threw myself at you anyway. I was shocked.'

'I was shocked, too,' he said drily, 'that I let you out of there instead of taking you to bed.'

'That's because you're a lovely man.' She beamed at him across the roof of the car. 'I have that on Hazel's authority. How did you manage to find a housekeeper so devoted to you?'

'I'm undemanding, easy-going, considerate, kind and——' he grinned at her snort of scepticism '—I pay top rates.'

Patrick took off his flying jacket and pushed it into his bag. Then he put on his suit jacket and, looking over at Darcie, gave a mocking little grin as he tweaked his tie straight.

In the dark grey suit, pale blue shirt—he looked marvellous! Darcie felt a small pang for the lousy suits that attracted lint like a magnet attracted filings, for the shirts with the too-tight collars, and the Paisley ties. She hadn't known it, but those clothes had been offering her an insight into a younger, brasher Patrick Stafford. 'Oh, darn it, Patrick,' she wailed, 'I *liked* it when I thought you had lousy taste. I enjoyed fixing your ties and tidying you up. I felt *needed*.'

'I gambled on it,' he said, unrepentant. 'By the time my luggage turned up, Fitzgibbon was hanging around, so—I decided I had more distinction as the worst-dressed man in town. You might have been going dancing with the racing romeo, but you were choosing my shirts.'

'The master strategist,' she said tartly.

'It's called hanging on by your fingernails,' he told her, and it appeased her.

She drove from the aerodrome and they talked and laughed, and Patrick hooked an arm over the back of her seat and angled himself so that he could watch her.

'About Fitzgibbon . . .?' he said.

'Ah, Fitz.' She smiled. 'He's handsome and dashing and loads of fun and, yes, he reminds me of Gavin in some ways, and we have a lot in common and can talk for hours, all night even, about racing and cars——'

'OK, OK. Sorry I asked.'

'But I wasn't looking for someone like Gavin,' she said softly. 'There *is* no one like Gavin. And there is no one like you.'

The car came to a rest at a red light and Patrick took her hand, raising it to his lips as he had once before. And as the traffic lights changed to green he released her and said, 'I love you, Darcie.'

They were a technicality, but the sweetest words of all. The car lunged across the intersection.

'Oh, Patrick,' she laughed, eyes shining. 'You *do* have some pretty words, after all.'

'I need you,' he told her, and she muffed the gear change.

'And I want you,' he said, very convincingly. The car lurched around a corner. 'For heaven's sake pull over before I say something we'll both regret.'

She laughed. 'Is there anything left to say?'

'Yes, there is. Pull over.'

'Yes, sir.'

She eased into a No Waiting zone and turned to Patrick. He slipped a hand to the back of her neck and turned her face to him, studying her with great solemnity. 'I've been managing my life for a long time, but make no mistake, I need you. Maybe not to reform my lousy tastes in clothes, or even to tidy me up, but I need you. You brought me home yesterday. I need you to bring me home every day,' he said softly.

Darcie traced a fingertip over his craggy chin, gently touched his scratches and bruises. Such an asymmetrical face he had. Such a tough, marvellous face, with eyes that didn't quite match, but which, between them, gave all the clues to the man. No use trying to decide which messages were the right ones. They all were. She could spend years reading them all. Years and years. 'Then I will,' she said.

Patrick cleared his throat. 'Do you like *Madame Butterfly?*' he asked, but as she frowned at this irrelevancy a truck driver, trapped behind them, gave a few deafening blasts on his horn. Darcie drove on.

'*Madame Butterfly?*' she repeated. 'I can take it in small doses. Why?'

'Racing drivers are such philistines.' He cleared his throat again and broke into 'One Fine Day'. His singing voice was powerful, an exaggerated, mock-operatic baritone with a torturous vibrato. After a few bars, mercifully he stopped, and looked enquiringly at her. 'Well?'

Darcie began to giggle. A fine, upstanding figure of a man, she'd said she wanted, one with twins in his family, one who could sing in tune to the children. 'Well—I'm tone deaf, but it sounds all right to me.'

'Well, then,' he said, taking a firm, precautionary grip on the armrest, 'will you marry me, sweetheart?'

'Oh, yes.' The car lurched to the right.

'Women drivers!' Patrick said.

They left the main traffic behind, and travelled along quiet back streets until the gleam of water appeared through the trees.

'Where are we going?' he asked.

'Somewhere secluded,' she said.

'Good.'

'A place where you can be yourself.'

'In that case . . .' He took off his tie, rolled it up and stuck it in his pocket.

'A place where you can do something you've wanted to do for just ages . . .' Patrick grinned wolfishly, and unfastened the collar button of his shirt. The Rolls came to rest in a riverside reserve. Ducks gabbled and gossiped in reeds along the bank. The grass was long between the swings, and the roundabout creaked as the light breeze pushed at it. 'For about thirty years, in fact.'

Patrick laughed softly. He took her hand and they walked across the park, stopping to kiss and stand awhile in each other's arms, murmuring promises for other places. And eventually they reached the roundabout.

Harlequin romances are now available in stores at these convenient times each month.

Harlequin Presents **Harlequin American Romance** **Harlequin Historical** **Harlequin Intrigue**	These series will be in stores on the 4th of every month.
Harlequin Romance **Harlequin Temptation** **Harlequin Superromance** **Harlequin Regency Romance**	New titles for these series will be in stores on the 16th of every month.

We hope this new schedule is convenient for you. With only two trips each month to your local bookseller, you will always be sure not to miss any of your favorite authors!

Happy reading!

Please note there may be slight variations in on-sale dates in your area due to differences in shipping and handling.

HDATES

Take 4 bestselling love stories FREE

Plus get a FREE surprise gift!

Special Limited-time Offer

Harlequin Reader Service®

Mail to

In the U.S.
3010 Walden Avenue
P.O. Box 1867
Buffalo, N.Y. 14269-1867

In Canada
P.O. Box 609
Fort Erie, Ontario
L2A 5X3

YES! Please send me 4 free Harlequin Presents® novels and my free surprise gift. Then send me 6 brand-new novels every month, which I will receive months before they appear in bookstores. Bill me at the low price of $2.24* each—a savings of 26¢ apiece off cover prices. There are no shipping, handling or other hidden costs. I understand that accepting the books and gift places me under no obligation ever to buy any books. I can always return a shipment and cancel at any time. Even if I never buy another book from Harlequin, the 4 free books and the surprise gift are mine to keep forever.

*Offer slightly different in Canada— $2.24 per book plus 69¢ per shipment for delivery. Sales tax applicable in N.Y.

306 BPA U103 (CAN)

106 BPA CAP7 (US)

Name _____ (PLEASE PRINT)

Address _____ Apt. No. _____

City _____ State/Prov. _____ Zip/Postal Code _____

This offer is limited to one order per household and not valid to present Harlequin Presents® subscribers. Terms and prices are subject to change.

© 1990 Harlequin Enterprises Limited

**In December,
let Harlequin warm your heart with the
AWARD OF EXCELLENCE title**

Harlequin Presents...

PENNY JORDAN

AWARD OF EXCELLENCE

a rekindled passion

Over twenty years ago, Kate had a holiday
affair with Joss Bennett and found herself
pregnant as a result. Believing that Joss had
abandoned her to return to his wife and child,
Kate had her daughter and made no attempt
to track Joss down.

At her daughter's wedding, Kate suddenly
confronts the past in the shape of the
bridegroom's distant relative—Joss. He quickly
realises that Sophy must be his daughter and
wonders why Kate never contacted him.

Can love be rekindled after twenty years?
Be sure not to miss this AWARD OF EXCELLENCE
title, available wherever Harlequin books
are sold.

HP-KIND-1